DAYBREAK ON RAVEN ISLAND

DAYBREAK ON RAVEN ISLAND

Fleur Bradley

VIKING

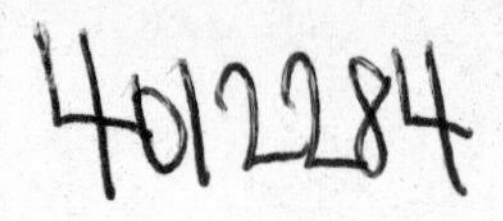

VIKING
An imprint of Penguin Random House LLC, New York

First published in the United States of America by Viking,
an imprint of Penguin Random House LLC, 2022

Visit us online at penguinrandomhouse.com.

Library of Congress Cataloging-in-Publication Data is available.

Manufactured in Canada

ISBN 9780593404638

10 9 8 7 6 5 4 3 2 1

FRI

Design by Lucia Baez · Text set in TT Chocolates

RAVEN ISLAND WAS A FORGOTTEN PLACE. Sure, you could see the massive rock from the Pacific coast. On a clearer day, you may get a glimpse of the prison, or the empty dock that used to welcome boats and ferries. You could even see the lighthouse, once proud and bright but now extinguished. Forgotten.

The ravens were perfectly fine with this situation. It was nice and quiet without humans. People could be noisy, and they'd just shoo the ravens away or give them a slightly terrified look. Ravens were dark and scary to people. Here on the island, they got to live in uninterrupted peace.

Without the humans around, it was easy to forget that Raven Island was once the site of a supermax prison, the kind of place you sent the toughest, most dangerous criminals. Like Big Mickey, that notorious mobster no prison seemed to be able to tame—he was sent to Raven Island back in the 1930s for multiple murders and racketeering. He got sick and died there. And there were dozens of stories just like his. Raven Island Prison was not a happy place.

One Friday morning, the oldest raven sat perched on the bell tower of the prison—her favorite spot. And she'd earned that prime location fair and square: she was the leader. The owner (more on her later) of Raven Island called her Poe—after the author Edgar Allan Poe—even though ravens didn't normally take on names. Poe was female, which the owner didn't know.

But Poe was proud of her name. She was the leader, so she was special.

The wind was steady and soft on the island. It was deceptive: the weather felt nice, and the sun was even peeking through the clouds to warm the land, the prison, and the bell tower where the raven was perched.

But you could feel it coming if you stood on Raven Island. You didn't have to be a smart raven to sense it was on its way.

Trouble. Change, too, though that felt different, a little more hopeful, if you were so inclined.

Poe felt her talons stiffen as the temperature shifted. And she didn't like change, not particularly. She preferred quiet, for herself and for the other ravens that called the island home.

Only now there were visitors coming.

It was bad enough that the owner, Ms. Chavez, was already here, along with that other human. Never mind the ghosts of Raven Island—they were stirring in their graves. Not that they liked to stay buried. Especially not at night.

But the ravens didn't mind the dead. It was the living they had to watch out for.

It was why Poe sat on the bell tower: to protect the dead. The humans had long forgotten about these ghosts—prisoners were the castaways of the world. But the ravens didn't think so. The ravens never forgot the dead. People would sometimes confuse the birds as a bad omen. Legend had it that ravens were the keepers of lost souls. And Raven Island had its share of those.

Out on the water, still far away but approaching rapidly, visitors were coming. Children, to make matters worse.

Didn't they know that Raven Island was no place for kids?

The ferry was already fighting the current and the choppy waters. The waves were slapping against the hull, telling the visitors not to come. But they weren't listening. Another half an hour and they would be here, on Raven Island.

If you were a bird expert, you would be able to observe Poe's discomfort. The way she adjusted her talons, then stretched her wings and flew away to join the others.

But the kid visitors on their way to Raven Island were no bird experts.

If only there was a way to tell them to stay away from Raven Island . . .

I

The Arrival

1
Friday, 9:45 a.m.

TORI WAS SO ANGRY, SHE FELT like she wanted to kick something. Preferably a soccer ball, but right there on the school bus, all she had were the metal bars under the seat in front of her.

And kicking those got her a nasty look from Liam, who was sitting in front of her. "Tori, you mind?"

Tori flipped her brown braided hair back and glared at Liam with her pale blue eyes. She knew she should've apologized, but she just couldn't get herself to do it. So Tori shrugged. She was tall and muscular, built to play soccer. She knew Liam would rather let it go than pick a fight.

"Everyone!" Mr. Thompson raised his voice, like all the seventh graders on the bus couldn't hear him. "Find your buddies!"

Tori thought the whole buddy system on a school field trip was kind of ridiculous. All it did was make everyone feel like they had to prove that they had a friend—and if you got left behind, it looked like *no one* wanted to be your friend.

Like Noah, the new kid. He sat up front, next to Mr. Thompson. He was the odd one out without a buddy, so he got to hang out with the teacher.

Tori called his name. "Hey, Noah." But the bus was so rowdy, he couldn't hear.

Tori's friends—or was it former friends?—were at a soccer tournament right now. Last month, she planned to be out there with them. But with her failing grades and *unruly behavior* (Mr. Thompson's words), she was benched and off the soccer team for the foreseeable future. Tori felt like an outsider.

So much for their team motto: *No one gets left behind.* Tori could practically hear the calls on the soccer field and feel the ball smack against her palms as she defended the goal.

No more of that.

"Noah!" she called again. He was one of the few Black kids in class, and he was always by himself. Tori wanted to turn her anger into something better and have him join her and her assigned buddy, Marvin. But Noah had his earbuds in.

Tori imagined her friends, huddling before the game.

In all fairness, her best friend and soccer teammate, Tanika, offered to tutor her to get her grades back up, but Tori refused. They barely hung out anymore, and Tori used to practically live at Tanika's house. It was Tori's choice. She just didn't know how to act without telling Tanika the truth about what was going on. And Tori wasn't ready to do that, not yet.

So now here she was, on this field trip rather than playing soccer. And she got paired with Marvin, who just kept his nose in a comic book the whole time. Some buddy.

She itched to get off the bus (Tori was the type who liked to keep moving), but with Mr. Thompson keeping an extra eye on her, it was better to get off last.

"Stick with your buddy!" Mr. Thompson hollered from outside the bus. They were at the ferry dock, waiting to get on.

Tori hoped she could find a spot outside. This bus was making her feel dizzy—there was no air, and nowhere to go.

Finally, the last of the seventh graders and the parent chaperones made it off the bus. Tori pulled herself up, ready to go.

Marvin was still hunched over, reading. Tori couldn't tell what the title was, only that Marvin was completely into the comic book.

"Yo, buddy!" Tori yelled. She was in a foul mood indeed. She was looking at a day of shuffling around, first onto the ferry, and then on this prison island. Any other day, she'd be all over a field trip. It was better than sitting in class, hands down. But right now, all she could think about was the soccer tournament she was going to miss, the chance to stand in front of the net and catch the ball.

"Hey, Marvin," Tori tried again. She knew she could be nicer. Marvin was a lone wolf: the only Korean kid in class, and since his best friend moved away, he mostly kept to himself. He was usually deep into a comic book or sketchbook. He wore a black beanie, pulled over his ears. Off in his own world. "We gotta get off this bus if we want to catch the ferry."

Marvin looked up, like he needed a minute to remember where he was. "Huh? Yeah, all right. The ferry." He smiled when he remembered where they were. "The prison!"

"Yeah." Tori resisted the urge to roll her eyes at his absentmindedness. "Come on."

They all took their backpacks and made their way off the bus. Noah stood all alone in the back of the crowd. Tori thought of calling him over to join her and Marvin, but Mr. Thompson gave her a stern look.

"Everyone!" Someone really needed to tell Mr. Thompson to stop yelling. He did it so often that people were beginning to tune him out. Seventh graders had a knack for that.

Tori shuffled onto the ferry and found a spot at the front. Marvin followed her; his walk was slow and bouncy, like he had a tune that he was dancing to inside his head.

"You want to sit inside?" he asked Tori.

They both looked at the crowded space.

"I'm fine out here." Tori was relieved to find a seat outside, despite the cold wind and cloudy weather. There were a few other kids out there—probably happy to get fresh air, too.

Tori looked out onto the water. A few miles into the Pacific, there was Raven Island. She thought she spotted a bird, though she couldn't be entirely sure.

"It's weird," Marvin said next to her.

"What—the island?" Tori asked. From where they sat, you couldn't really make out the prison, but an old stone mansion was clearly visible.

"This field trip is weird," Marvin said. "Last-minute, to some abandoned prison on an island. Why let a bunch of seventh graders run around if you kept it all locked up for so long?"

Marvin was right: that was odd. But before Tori could say anything, there was a loud foghorn.

Weird or not, they were off to Raven Island.

2
Friday, 9:55 a.m.

NOAH WANTED TO TELL MR. THOMPSON that the buddy system was a bad idea. Because if there are thirty-one kids in a class and they all pair up, you will have one left. It was basic math.

Noah ended up being the extra kid. He saw it coming. Not that anyone picked on him a lot; he was just ignored, forgotten. Noah didn't have any friends because he and his dad moved to town in the middle of seventh grade. Everyone already had their friends picked out. On top of that, Noah was quiet and wore no-brand clothes.

The perfect recipe to yield no friends.

As a result, Mr. Thompson was Noah's buddy, which was worse than being alone. Noah heard some kids snicker while they were still at school and everyone had already paired off. Aside from the fact that it was totally embarrassing to Noah, Mr. Thompson (who was very frazzled) kept forgetting they were buddies.

They were on the ferry, inside this giant covered space with hard benches. It smelled like salty ocean water and fish. Noah took out his earbuds.

"Oh, right, Noah." Mr. Thompson rubbed his head. "Listen,

why don't you buddy up with Tristan and Liam over there?"

Tristan and Liam both made a face—it was just for a split second, but Noah saw it and wished he could hang out with anyone but these two kids today. Tristan and Liam weren't known for their friendliness. And everyone knew that three is a crowd. Apparently, everyone except for Mr. Thompson.

"Marvin is over there," Noah said as he clutched his notebook. Marvin was alone most of the time, too. Through the giant windows on the ferry, he saw Marvin out there on one of the benches, his beanie pulled over his ears.

"Okay, just let him know you're his buddy now." Mr. Thompson had already turned his attention to his clipboard. "Last-minute field trip," he muttered before walking away. "Such a great idea."

It had been Mrs. Heinemann who had organized the field trip—she was old friends with Raven Island's owner, Ms. Chavez, who had called her personally to set up the seventh-grade trip. Why Ms. Chavez had chosen this particular class, no one really knew . . . It was all very mysterious.

But when Mrs. Heinemann caught a stomach bug, Mr. Thompson was put in charge. It was clear to Noah that Mr. Thompson was struggling to keep everyone in line *and* be his buddy.

When Tristan sent another sideways glance in his direction, Noah went outside. He didn't need a buddy, especially not those guys.

The horn blew, and Noah felt the ferry shift under his feet.

He hated field trips. And he hated the outdoors even more. He used to love to get outside on weekends, hiking with his mom and dad. But now that his mom was gone, he and his dad mostly got pizza and had movie marathons. Noah could tell his dad was having a hard time, too.

Outside on the ferry deck, he could feel the Pacific Ocean's water spray his face. Noah closed his eyes and imagined he was home in his room, working on his latest science experiment. He was studying the behavior of ants; he even had a giant colony he was observing in a glass terrarium. His dad wasn't too fond of it, but Noah made sure not to let any of the ants get out. He was a scientist, like his mom. Careful, meticulous.

Noah sat down on the bench, a few feet away from Marvin but close enough that it might look like they were buddies. That way, Mr. Thompson wouldn't ask any questions.

Noah zipped up his hoodie and crossed his arms to stay warm. He didn't have a jacket because he'd just moved north from San Diego. He was afraid to tell his dad he needed one because he always seemed so preoccupied with work. Noah was already freezing, and they were barely halfway into the ferry trip. The cold ocean water stung his bare shins under his too-short pants.

The waves hit the ferry's hull like a warning drumbeat. Noah had read up on the island a little and knew that the currents were deadly out here. Back when the prison was still operational, a few convicts had escaped and drowned, drifting out into the vast Pacific Ocean, never to be seen again. Those currents were no joke. The ferry could only make one trip twice a day: during two hours in the morning and two in the afternoon.

Noah looked up at the island ahead. He could make out the prison now, the giant brick building with the bell tower at its center. There was a bird up there.

A raven. It was looking at Noah, telling him he wasn't welcome.

Noah opened his notebook and took a pen out of his backpack's side pocket. He wrote down *ravens*. The book was for writing down things that made him afraid. The idea (his therapist's) was that the act of writing it down would make him less scared. So far, it wasn't working.

Noah blinked, and the raven was gone.

"Dude, did you see that bird?" Marvin said next to him.

Noah was about to open his mouth when Tori answered instead. "It's a raven." Of course Marvin was talking to Tori, his buddy. Not to Noah.

Tori went on, "Apparently there are about a dozen of them living on the island. They're the protectors."

Noah knew that, too; he'd read about it. There were thirteen ravens on Raven Island, to be exact. Rumor had it that their wings were clipped by the owner so that they couldn't leave. But Noah didn't feel like he was part of this conversation, so he kept his findings to himself.

Noah twisted the watch on his wrist. It was a gift from his mom; the watch had been his grandpa's. It was old but still worked.

"Protectors, huh?" Marvin said. "Long as they don't attack my head, they can go on protecting the island all they want."

"They're protecting the ghosts," Noah said before he remembered he was trying to stay invisible. Noah was about to explain that in folklore, ravens were seen as mediators between the living and dead worlds. On Raven Island, the story was that they protected the ghosts. But Tori and Marvin hadn't heard him anyway, not over the loud waves and the ferry's roaring engine.

Noah wrote down another thing he was afraid of: *disappearing*. Somehow, he figured that was very easy on Raven Island. It looked like it could just swallow you whole. And as much as Noah liked being invisible, disappearing entirely scared him.

But then he thought of his mom. What if being on the island could bring Noah closer to her? What if he could meet his mom's ghost? Could the ravens help him?

Noah closed his notebook, and he suddenly felt hopeful for the first time in a while. Maybe this trip to Raven Island wasn't such a bad idea after all.

The ferry horn blew. They had arrived on Raven Island. And little did Noah know that he was wrong. Visiting here was a very bad idea indeed.

Because the island wasn't going to let the kids go.

Not without a fight.

3
Friday, 10:00 a.m.

MARVIN WAS ONE OF THE FEW kids from Greenville Middle School who was actually excited to go to Raven Island. Sure, the place was old and abandoned, and the sky looked like it might pour all day, but it was an abandoned prison! With a lighthouse! And who knows what other ghostly stuff . . .

See, Marvin was making a horror movie, and he desperately needed a ghostly setting with lots of ghosts and mysterious past. Ideally, the ghosts of Raven Island would show up for his movie. Marvin had skimmed a little of the island's history online the day before. The place was supposed to be super haunted. And Marvin wanted to shoot some footage with his phone while they were there. It was just a bummer that they weren't there at night . . .

Only they weren't allowed to use their phones. And Mr. Thompson was a real stickler for rules. But Marvin thought he might sneak in some footage when Mr. Thompson wasn't looking.

Indie MovieFest was happening later in the summer, and every year there was a contest that kids could submit short films to. Marvin was determined to create something amazing. He didn't know what it would be yet, but he knew it would be great.

The plan had been to make the movie and go to Indie MovieFest with Kevin, his best friend. But Kevin moved away at the beginning of the school year, and now he barely answered Marvin's texts anymore. Never mind Kevin—Marvin would just make the movie by himself. Not that Marvin didn't have other friends; they were just not close ones.

Marvin was forever overlooked at home. Noah and Marvin had this in common, but they didn't know that yet. Between Marvin's loud older twin sisters, who were always talking about their college applications and graduation, his mom and dad's stories about the family restaurant (Korean fusion—it had, like, a gazillion stars on all the restaurant review sites), and his grandma, who only spoke Korean and mostly ignored everyone, Marvin often felt forgotten. But if he made a cool horror movie for Indie MovieFest, maybe he would finally be listened to. Maybe everyone at home wouldn't just be talking about him when he got in trouble (which was more often than Marvin cared to admit).

From afar, Raven Island looked dark and creepy. There was the lighthouse, sticking out from the top. The pine trees looked almost black, and the rocks practically told them to go away. The island looked almost like a mirage, even though it wasn't warm at all. There was a low-hanging fog that seemed to eat the island up.

And when the ferry dipped, the island just . . . disappeared. Only to pop back up out of nowhere.

"Like *The Twilight Zone*," Marvin murmured to himself. He was a huge fan of the show—both the old version and the new, revamped one from one of his favorite directors, Jordan Peele. Still. It was one thing to watch it on TV; quite another to visit a place like it.

His buddy, Tori, was all right. Although Marvin could see she didn't want to be there. He'd heard she was suspended from the soccer team because of her grades. That had to stink. And now her team was at a soccer tournament without her. Of course she was upset about being on this field trip.

Marvin tried to hide his excitement around Tori, but now that they were getting closer, he was craning his neck to see.

The prison looked crumbled and abandoned, even from afar. Marvin thought he could use this view in the opening credits of his movie. He really wanted to film at night, but maybe he could use a filter . . .

When the ferry docked, the horn blew and the kids filed off the boat. Marvin tucked his comic book into his backpack.

Tori sighed, and they both got up. That new kid (Nathan? No, his name was Noah.) also got to his feet, but sort of hung back. It was a little weird.

With Tori dragging her feet, the three of them were the last to step off the ferry, so as they climbed the stairs from the dock to the island, all they saw was their classmates' backs. But once they got up there . . .

It was like one of Marvin's scarier comics, only this was real life. The prison was built out of bricks, but you could tell that it hadn't been well maintained, because there was moss all over and vines growing halfway up the walls. The building was like an octopus, with a center body that stood tall and had a bell tower, and from that center there were long, tentacle-like hallways. Mr. Thompson had told Marvin and the other students the day before that there were five hallways during his introduction to Raven Island.

This was so cool! And creepy. It was even better than he imagined, as a setting for his movie . . .

Marvin was bouncing on his heels as his mind raced. There were some good possibilities here. Marvin wanted to be famous, like M. Night Shyamalan, Alfred Hitchcock, and Jennifer Kent (he loved *The Babadook*)—Marvin dreamed of being the next Korean horror legend! Maybe he would even be the first. He just needed to shoot a film on Raven Island.

Not that there was any reception out here.

Maybe when Mr. Thompson isn't looking, Marvin thought. *Later . . .*

There were clusters of kids all over the open area outside the prison. Each kid looked cold and tired. The chaperone parents who were supposed to watch the whole class were mostly hanging out with their own kids and also looked sleepy. It was the end of the school year, when your pencils were stubby and your notebooks crumpled, and your backpack smelled like a hundred different lunches. Who could blame them for wanting to be somewhere else?

And Mr. Thompson looked about done, too. "Gather around! Find your buddy!"

There were groans. Tori rolled her eyes as Marvin walked back and stood awkwardly next to her. That kid Noah was way in the back.

"We'll be going inside the prison as one big group, to save time," Mr. Thompson said as everyone settled down. "After that, we'll have lunch here, in the field. And remember, everyone: we have to catch the ferry at two o'clock. Otherwise, we're stuck here on Raven Island until tomorrow."

"Cool," someone said in the back of the crowd.

"No, *not* cool," Mr. Thompson said. "Once again: the ferry leaves at two." He looked so grumpy, no one dared speak up. "The buddy system will make sure we all leave on time. And I'll be doing roll call. No stragglers! We'll meet right here, in the field."

Marvin looked at the ground. If this was once a field, grass had long ago given up and died. All he saw was dirt. And maybe bird poo.

"You all have your maps." Mr. Thompson looked at his clipboard. "Not that you'll need them, because you won't be going into the woods or to the lighthouse or the owner's mansion. And no phones."

Or what? Marvin thought. He was really hoping to check out the lighthouse. He'd overheard one of his classmates mention that it was haunted.

"This is going to be a long day," Tori muttered.

Marvin pretended to agree. "But you gotta admit: this prison is looking dynamite . . ."

Tori frowned. " 'Nasty' is more like it."

Marvin was about to tell her it could be cool on the inside when this lady came walking up. He froze.

The lady was older and Hispanic, short—maybe five feet tall

by Marvin's reckoning. She was so skinny and pale, for a second, he thought she might be a ghost—they did say the island was haunted. She wore black pinstriped slacks and a black shirt, buttoned all the way to her neck. She also wore these rain boots that totally ruined her authoritative look. Her hair was dark with silver strands, very straight and to her shoulders.

The most intimidating part was her pale face and her piercing dark eyes. Marvin realized he'd been holding his breath and slowly let it out.

The whole class was silent, which only really happened when the school principal showed up.

"Welcome to Raven Island," the lady said in a soft-spoken voice, rolling the letter *R*. "My name is Melody Chavez."

4
Friday, 10:45 a.m.

NOAH HELD HIS BREATH. YOU COULD hear a pin drop. The whole seventh-grade class stood still and stayed silent; Mr. Thompson's mouth was hanging open in shock.

Noah knew why: Ms. Chavez owned the island—creepy prison, birds, and all. Her father had been the prison warden right before the place shut down, back in 1972. Ms. Chavez used to be a super successful lawyer, and so she bought the place after it closed. Ms. Chavez looked like she really, *really* didn't like the sun.

Noah hung back, half hiding behind Tori now, who was somewhat taller than him and all muscle from playing soccer for years. He felt safe.

"I'm the owner of this building and the island you're standing on," Ms. Chavez said. A few people looked at their feet, including Noah. "And I'm also the person who invited your class to come here, to the first-ever private tour of the Raven Island Prison. I am hoping we can move on from its tragically dark history and bring Raven Island back into the sun," she said as she spread her arms and tried to smile warmly.

Noah couldn't help but notice that this place didn't get much sun—in fact, the clouds looked like they were gathering steam to maybe dump a few gazillion gallons of water on them all. Which would be bad for Noah, since he was very much underdressed for this field trip already.

Ms. Chavez said, "I wish to make a change. And it starts by inviting people back to Raven Island." She paused. "Mr. Thorne, your tour guide, will tell you all about its history."

Mr. Thompson cleared his throat. "Thank you, Ms. Chavez, for graciously inviting us to your island. We"—he threw an urgent glance at all the kids—"will be on our best behavior today."

Ms. Chavez gave Mr. Thompson one of those intense stares that said she didn't really care, and then she turned and walked away. Everyone quickly began murmuring to each other.

But not Noah, Tori, and Marvin. The three of them watched Ms. Chavez walk into the forest, toward where the owner's mansion was, and the lighthouse, of course. But right before Ms. Chavez walked out of sight, she spread her arms. Two ravens swooped down and then flew back up into the trees.

Like Ms. Chavez was their master.

"*Duuuude,*" Marvin whispered. "You see that?"

"Yeah," Tori whispered back.

"Creepy," Noah added.

"Man, I wish I could use my phone to film," Marvin muttered.

Tori turned around. "Have you been standing there behind me the whole time?" she asked Noah.

Noah felt his face go beet red. He hated when that happened—it was why he hid and always tried to make himself as small as possible. "Yes," he said, his voice squeaky as a mouse. "Sorry."

Tori frowned. "Just get in front. You're creeping me out."

Noah did so, awkwardly.

"Hey, aren't you the extra kid?" Marvin asked Noah. "You got paired with the teacher for this buddy business, right?"

Noah nodded, not trusting his voice entirely.

"That's sad," Marvin said.

"Sad, for sure. Right up there with the whole ridiculous buddy system," Tori said. She reached inside her pocket and pulled out a ball. One of those stress balls, Noah thought. They had them at the counselor's office, he remembered from his first day. "I tried to call you on the bus, Noah," she said. "But you had your earbuds in."

Marvin said, "Just stick with me and Tori, Noah."

"Totally," Tori said. "No one gets left behind."

"Okay." Noah didn't want to tell them that he was already sticking with them. It was nice to be part of a group and actually be invited.

There was the scuttle of seventh graders following Mr. Thompson through the dirty metal door for the tour. Tori and Marvin hung back, which Noah didn't mind. He was seriously creeped out by this place and wasn't looking forward to being trapped in a dirty old prison.

Noah looked out over the water as they got in the very back of the line. He saw a boat, a smaller one than the enormous ferry they'd taken here to Raven Island. The boat was . . .

Coming this way!

Noah had excellent attention to detail and often picked up on things before others did—it was the one good thing that came with being on high alert all the time. "Check it out," he said to Tori and Marvin. "Look. There's a boat."

Marvin and Tori followed his gaze.

The boat made Noah feel anxious, though he couldn't say why. He almost pulled out his notebook and wrote it down, but knew Tori and Marvin would probably think that was odd. So he didn't. Noah focused on the boat and the way it was getting tossed around by the waves.

"That's weird," Tori said. "I thought we were the only ones getting a tour."

But there was no denying the boat's direction: it was definitely on its way to Raven Island, expected to arrive right before eleven, when the currents made it impossible to leave. Someone else was coming to visit the island.

The question was: Who?

5
Friday, 10:55 a.m.

TORI WATCHED THE BOAT ALONG WITH Marvin and Noah. It was out there on the choppy water, coming closer by the minute.

"It's definitely on its way here," Marvin said.

"I thought we were the first tour," Tori said. She shifted her weight from one leg to the other, something she did when she was guarding the goal or when she was antsy. She squeezed the stress ball, not that it was making her feel less stressed. But then at least she could tell the counselor she was using it. "What's it doing coming here?"

The class was slowly trickling in through the rusty metal door at the far end of one of the corridors. The prison looked like a giant spider, its long legs stretched in all directions.

Tori, Noah, and Marvin managed to hang back and get a better look at the boat approaching the island, but eventually they had to go inside. Tori glanced over her shoulder one last time. She wondered who else was coming to Raven Island.

Inside, the prison smelled like mold, dirt, and a little like sewage.

"Yo, who farted?" someone asked up ahead. But Tori knew this was just the smell of an abandoned building. The hallway was lined with prison cells, the metal bars closing off each empty cell. Water sat on some of the bunks, looking green and mossy. The cells still had stuff scribbled on the walls, though you couldn't make out what they said. Dirt and mold had covered up the words of the prison, like time had silenced the dead prisoners.

Tori shivered.

"You see that?" Noah asked behind her.

Tori jumped. Noah really had to learn not to sneak up on a person like that.

"What?" Tori was happy to have a reason to stop for a moment. She tucked the stress ball back into her pocket.

"There." Noah pointed to one of the cells. "Never mind," he added softly. "I thought I saw someone."

"This place has to be haunted," Marvin said. Then a couple of guys from class joined him and started discussing if ghosts were real or not. Marvin was one of those kids who was cool, easygoing, and friends with everyone. "Did you see the raven on the bell tower?" Marvin said as he was peering between the prison cell's bars. "The ravens protect the spirits."

"Stinky spirits," Tristan said as he wrinkled his nose.

Tori didn't believe in ghosts—she believed in what was real, what you could actually see. And what she saw was just a bunch of nasty space. "Let's go." She began to charge ahead—she figured Marvin and Noah would catch up.

Finally, they reached the end of the long hall of prison cells. There was a large dome-shaped space, with the bell tower up above. A thick rope was draped down from the bell and was held back by a large metal hook.

"What's the bell for?" Noah asked.

But he just got a stern look from Mr. Thompson. "Class! Please welcome Mr. Thorne, Raven Island's caretaker and, today, your tour guide."

A short, round man seemed to appear out of nowhere from behind Mr. Thompson. He wore a black uniform: a button-up jacket, black pants, and shiny black shoes. He had a black hat under his arm—when Tori saw that, she realized that he was dressed as a prison guard.

"Hello, seventh grade of"—Mr. Thorne paused and looked toward Mr. Thompson—"Greenville Middle School." Mr. Thompson tried a smile, but Mr. Thorne didn't reciprocate.

"Welcome to Raven Island. Welcome to the prison," he said gravely. Mr. Thorne looked very unhappy to be there. And he was even paler than Ms. Chavez. Like you could see right through him. "I am the caretaker of Raven Island." Mr. Thorne waved his short arms, like it was a beautiful sight. He sent the smell of cigarette smoke across the room.

Tori wrinkled her nose. Between the smell of Mr. Thorne and bird poo, it smelled even worse here in the bell tower.

The class stood in a circle around the room. Tori noticed for the first time in a while that her soccer teammates were very obviously missing. She wondered how the tournament was going. She imagined her friend Tanika passing the ball across the field to Jackie and then—

Tori shook her head to banish all thoughts of soccer and tried to focus on Mr. Thorne.

"You are a very special group," Mr. Thorne said. He was paler than a sheet of paper, and his eyes were super intense. "Anyone want to guess why?"

Someone yawned. The class was silent.

Mr. Thorne sighed. "You are the first group to visit the prison in over fifty years!" He paused, making a point to glance around the whole group. "You kids had better wake up, or the ghosts will get you."

There were some snickers, but Mr. Thorne was clearly very serious.

Mr. Thorne went on, "It is estimated that more than two thousand people died here on Raven Island."

That was very creepy. Everyone stood up a little straighter and paid attention.

"Before it became a prison, Raven Island was a military fort, then it was turned into a sanatorium over a hundred years ago." Mr. Thorne's voice echoed and swirled around the room. "It was designed to house more than two hundred people, sick with tuberculosis."

Liam laughed. "Basically, Raven Island is where you toss people you don't want. Like Noah." He gave Noah a light shove.

Tori felt her anger boil as she watched Noah shrink.

But before she could do anything about it, Marvin stepped forward. "No one thinks you're funny, Liam. Besides, Noah is with me and Tori."

Liam slunk back after Mr. Thompson gave him a warning look. And Noah stood a little straighter.

Tori took a breath and forced herself to calm down.

Mr. Thorne continued, "Each day, nurses would take the ferry just like you did this morning and arrive at exactly ten o'clock. They would pull twenty-four-hour shifts to avoid the currents."

The whole class listened. Well, almost everyone. Tori could see Marvin secretly stepping back behind her, reading that comic.

"This bell tower was built for a special purpose," Mr. Thorne said. "Can anyone guess why?"

It was silent for what seemed like forever.

"To ring it when someone died," Marvin said behind Tori, out of nowhere. So he was paying attention after all.

"Exactly," Mr. Thorne said.

Just then, a shadow seemed to swoop into the room, in the darkness behind Mr. Thorne.

The rope swung away from the hook. And the bell rang.

6
Friday, 11:30 a.m.

THE CLANGING OF THE GIANT BELL made Marvin's ears ring. It was amplified by the dome-shaped tower, making the sound so loud that he thought his brain might explode. Most of his classmates were covering their ears.

"Ha ha ha," a woman's voice went behind Mr. Thorne's back. You could barely hear her over the loud clanging bells.

Marvin rubbed his head. The bell sound seemed to be bouncing around inside his brain.

Suddenly, there was a guy who pushed his way past the class. He said to the prankster lady, "Come on, Tammy." Marvin thought he recognized the man from somewhere, but he couldn't place him . . . The guy pulled the bell ringer's arm, so she wasn't able to hide behind Mr. Thorne anymore.

The woman named Tammy (who rang the bell) was laughing. She was white and wore a hooded sweatshirt and a bright yellow headband in her brown hair.

"I apologize, kids," her friend said. He was tall with olive skin and had broad shoulders and black-framed glasses. He wore cargo pants, like he was ready to go on an adventure. "My name is Hatch."

"Oh, from *Ghost Catchers*!" Marvin said before he could

think. He grinned; Marvin had marathon-watched the first eight seasons and was eagerly awaiting the next one.

Hatch smiled. "Yeah, kid. You watch the show?"

Marvin shrugged. "Sometimes." It was the truth. *Ghost Catchers* was this online streaming show where Hatch and his crew would go to supposedly haunted places and try to collect evidence of ghosts. Marvin thought that their "evidence" could just as well be a shadow or some dust. But he wasn't about to say that now.

Hatch smiled in this fake way, like he would do on the show when he talked into the camera. He turned to the class. "Everyone: *Ghost Catchers* was just nominated for the Ghostly Award."

From their expressions, it was obvious that none of the kids knew what that award was.

"Are you here to film an episode?" Marvin asked. That would be pretty cool. Marvin always wanted to see a real film crew at work. Maybe he could learn a few things and tell Kevin about it. And maybe he could use what he learned to make his own movie better . . .

"We are," Hatch said. He looked at the woman who rang the bell. "In fact, we should get moving, Tammy."

"Yes, boss." Tammy disappeared behind the seventh-grade tour group.

Marvin could see another guy who was white, wearing a beanie like him and dressed in black—film people liked to look serious and dark, he guessed.

The guy was joined by Tammy, and they were hauling reels of power cords and giant crates on wheels. Marvin wished he could join them.

"That guy over there is our location scout," Hatch said when he saw the kids looking. "His name is . . . Well, I don't remember. But you may see him around the island. He'll uncover all its secrets." Hatch smiled.

Mr. Thorne didn't look very happy about that.

"His name is Bob, Hatch," Tammy said next to him.

"Right," Hatch said. Then he added in his bellowing on-screen voice, "My apologies for interrupting your tour."

Mr. Thorne looked annoyed. "We'll get back to it, then. Thank you."

Before leaving to join his crew, Hatch waved at the crowd of seventh graders, like he was the queen of England. Marvin rolled his eyes. Still. Film crews were way cooler than any field trip.

And Marvin felt an idea hatch (no pun intended) inside his brain. It was a bad idea probably, but then, didn't all great adventures start off that way?

Mr. Thorne muttered, "Well, I had no idea that there would be a film crew here today. That must've been Ms. Chavez's idea." He turned to the class and cleared his throat. "Back to the history of Raven Island Prison."

Marvin wasn't the best listener all the time, he knew that. He'd quickly get distracted, forget a few details, and then he'd fill in the rest with his imagination if he wasn't sure. That got him into trouble in history class, and never mind math, when he'd just fudge the answers.

Only this time, he didn't want to forget. He was actually interested in the stories of Raven Island Prison—and he didn't want to get it wrong. For his movie. Marvin was still developing his ideas, but Raven Island was stirring up some inspiration.

But Marvin didn't have a notebook or even a pen. He nudged Noah and whispered, "Give me your notebook."

But instead of handing it to Marvin, Noah clutched the notebook and pen. It was frayed at the edges, like he had been taking it everywhere. "Why?" Noah whispered back.

Mr. Thorne said, "Let's talk about the early prison break, during the first year Raven Island Prison was operational."

"I want to take notes," Marvin whispered. "At least tear me off some paper."

Noah shook his head at first. But then he opened to a blank page and handed the notebook to Marvin with a pen.

Marvin started writing, trying to keep up as Mr. Thorne told the story.

"The first year Raven Island Prison opened, the rules were still fairly relaxed. The theory was, if you were stuck on an island with currents that made it pretty much impossible to leave, where were you going to go?

"But two prisoners, one big man in for a bank robbery, one short guy convicted of money laundering, didn't come back from their daily run to the docks. One hour passed, then two. The ferry run was canceled. Raven Island was on lockdown.

"A day passed, but no one saw the two prisoners. A search party combed the island but came up empty.

"Then, on day three, two guards who were sent to look for the prisoners in the forest found something."

Mr. Thorne paused, and the whole seventh grade held its breath.

"What?" Marvin finally asked. His hand was cramping up from writing so fast, but he was dying to know.

Mr. Thorne waited another moment before he continued.

"The guards found shoes. Two pairs of prison-issued black lace-up shoes. They sat neatly under a tree, as if the two men had climbed the pine tree to escape by flying off the island."

"But that's not possible," Tori said. She sounded irritated.

Mr. Thorne seemed grumpy about being interrupted. "No talking, kids."

Tori huffed. But Marvin imagined that the two prisoners did fly away.

Like the ravens.

Mr. Thorne said softly, "But when the guards came back, the shoes were gone. Some say that the trees swallowed those two prisoners whole. That Raven Island took its bounty. Every year, the prisoners would place a pair of shoes by the forest. And every year, they disappeared."

"*Duuuude,*" someone whispered in the back.

Mr. Thorne added in a grumpy voice, "Just don't think you kids can go into the forest. It's off-limits!"

The class was silent.

"Or Raven Island will take its bounty," Mr. Thorne added in a dark voice.

But Marvin was already hatching a plan. He didn't know how yet, but he was determined to sneak into the forest . . .

Haunted or not.

7
Friday, 12:15 p.m.

TORI DID HER BEST TO PAY attention to the tour, but it was hard to hear Mr. Thorne speak when she was all the way in the back. They walked all five halls, looking inside more prison cells than she hoped to encounter in a lifetime.

Seeing these tiny spaces with bars made her feel like there was a giant gorilla sitting on her chest. She couldn't help but think of her brother. Was this how he was living?

Surely modern prisons had to have better conditions. Tori wasn't sure—she had yet to visit her brother.

She tried to imagine the spirits, if there were any.

Were they dead prisoners? People who died from tuberculosis? It was a cold and sad place, this prison. Tori couldn't wait to get outside, even if it was cold and wet.

Mr. Thorne stopped in the last hall and turned around, looking grave. "In this hall is cell fourteen. It is rumored that during the time when this was a sanatorium, every patient who stayed there died. The doctors eventually closed off this room, and it wasn't reopened until tuberculosis had a vaccine, the sanatorium was closed, and Raven Island became a prison."

The class was silent.

Tori felt curious enough to ask, "Then what happened? Did every prisoner in there die?"

Mr. Thorne paused, milking the silence for all it was worth. "Eventually, yes. It's been said that the dead prisoners from cell fourteen still haunt the halls. And when it's raining, you can hear moans, screams of pain, and crying from this cell."

"Creepy," Marvin muttered next to Tori.

Tori thought it was immensely sad instead. She felt like she couldn't breathe.

Suddenly, there was a black-and-white shadow near the ground.

"*Arghhh!*" Mr. Thorne exclaimed.

Tori almost lost her balance as she jumped.

"It's just a cat," Noah said. He leaned down to pet the cat, who was black and white, looking like he was wearing a tuxedo. "He's sweet."

Tori sneezed. "I'm allergic."

Mr. Thorne had found his composure. "This is Mr. Hitchcock, our island cat named after filmmaker Alfred Hitchcock. He's here to catch the mice."

Just like that, the cat darted away.

Mr. Thorne said, "It has been claimed that when Mr. Hitchcock shows, the spirit of the last prison warden follows."

There was a heavy silence.

Mr. Thorne added, "The warden goes around chasing people into the prison cells. And then he slams the bars."

More silence.

Suddenly, a loud *bang* came from down the hall.

The sound of the prison cell closing.

Tori jumped again. Thankfully, her soccer training made her

quick on her feet. Was this the prison warden, trying to tell them to go away?

"Yo—was that the prison warden's ghost?" Marvin asked next to her, obviously wondering the same thing, but he sounded way too happy for Tori's liking.

The class erupted in talking and amazed exclamations.

"Silence!" Mr. Thorne yelled. But you could tell he was shaken, too. "The prison warden has been known to haunt Raven Island. So watch your backs, kids. Or you'll end up locked inside cell fourteen . . ."

That scared seventh grade into silence. Tori felt a cold breeze down her neck. She shivered.

"Now, the last big event of Raven Island: the escape of three prisoners in 1972, the year the prison closed down for good because it became too expensive to operate." Mr. Thorne's face seemed to cloud over as he continued the story. "Three prisoners, brothers Robert and John Smith, and John Bellini, managed to get themselves assigned to late-night laundry duty, for good behavior. You have to remember: Raven Island was thought of as the ultimate security prison. There was no way on or off the island without layers and layers of security. The three men were relatively free to move about the prison as part of the laundry detail. And they hatched a plan, together, even though the two Smith brothers were hardly friendly with their fellow prisoner John Bellini. The Smith brothers were doing their best to stay out of trouble. John Bellini was . . . a darker sort."

The class was silent, hanging on to Mr. Thorne's every word.

"All three sneaked out unbeknownst to the guards by using

dirty guards' uniforms and walking right through the prison gates." Mr. Thorne took a breath. "Of course, they still needed to get off Raven Island. From the prison cells," he said, pointing down the hall, "they had a perfect view of the rocky beach near the ferry dock. There was a boat moored there and forgotten. The three men took it and tried to row to shore." He paused.

The class was silent, waiting for the story to continue.

"Did they make it?" Tori asked, fearing what the answer was.

Mr. Thorne shook his head but looked puzzled, like maybe he wasn't sure. "No one knows exactly what happened. However, it is thought that the warden tried to retrieve the boat with the prisoners, but all drowned in the process. The prisoners are presumed dead. The warden's body washed ashore a few days after the attempted prison break."

"Well, that's depressing," someone said in the back. It was true, though.

Mr. Thorne grumbled, then said, "Let's wrap up our tour, shall we?"

Tori reached inside her pocket and squeezed the stress ball, but she had a hard time letting go of her feelings.

The class ate their lunches standing up—the dirt field was not exactly inviting to sit on. It was now after noon. Just under two hours until she could ditch this stupid island, Tori thought. This had to be the worst (and coldest!) field trip ever.

She managed to eat half of her sandwich, made by her dad. As a construction foreman, he was up early and made everyone lunches before making her mom breakfast, for when she got back from her night shift as an EMT. But the sandwich just made her think of home, and how things were so quiet without her brother Danny. Her dad tried to make her feel better by putting some cookies (chocolate chip, her favorite) in her lunch box, but Tori wasn't hungry. She was putting her lunch in her backpack when she noticed Marvin pointing to the trees.

"You guys see that?" Marvin said.

"Huh?" Noah squinted. He had some peanut butter stuck in the corner of his mouth.

Tori didn't see anything.

"I just saw a dude in old-timey prison clothing," Marvin said. "He walked into the woods."

Tori wasn't convinced. "Maybe it's a ghost," she said sarcastically.

"Yeah, maybe it is," Marvin said, oblivious to her tone. He tucked his comic into the side pocket of his backpack. "I'm gonna go see."

Noah hesitated only a moment before following him, but Tori stayed where she was. She didn't really want to leave the class, since she didn't want to miss the ferry.

But then she thought she saw it, too. A shadow of a person. It was hiding behind a tree.

Looking. Watching. It creeped Tori out, but made her curious, too. But then the forest swallowed the shadow up, and it was gone.

Who was that?

"Wait up," Tori said to Marvin and Noah. "I'm coming."

8

Friday, 12:45 p.m.

NOAH REALLY DIDN'T WANT TO LEAVE the group, but he figured Marvin was his buddy now, after Marvin stood up for him earlier. And Noah wasn't about to let him run off on his own.

Then Noah saw the figure, too—right there past the trees. The man wore prison stripes, the kind Noah had only seen in old movies from the sixties, with his dad.

"Help!" a voice went. "Save me!" It came from a different direction, deep in the woods.

Noah froze. "You hear that?" he whispered.

Only Tori had passed him already, jogging ahead. "Let's check it out. Come on, Noah."

The figure was gone. And there were no more cries for help.

Noah couldn't help but wonder: Was this one of the ghosts of Raven Island? Noah wasn't sure if he believed in ghosts. He believed in facts, numbers, things you could quantify. Things you could see.

And yet . . .

After his mom died, Noah still talked to her every night, just like they'd always done. He'd tell her about his day, and how he and his dad were trying to make the best of it now that she was gone. He'd tell her about the rest of the family—how they got together every Sunday for dinner now that Noah and his dad had moved closer, and how his aunts and uncles still had lively debates at the table. But also, how that made him miss her even more, because she wasn't there to join the conversation.

Every night, Noah could swear his mom was there, sitting on the edge of his bed. He could feel her in the room. Was that her ghost? Noah wasn't sure.

He did know that he was beginning to forget her. First, he wasn't sure how her smile looked anymore—he'd had to check the photo album to remember. And lately, he'd forgotten what her laugh sounded like. He really missed talking science with her, too. Noah's mom had been a lab chemist, working on developing new medicine. She was awesome.

But memories of his mom were slipping away, and there wasn't anything he could do to stop it. Holding on to her memories was like holding water in your hands: sooner or later it all poured out.

It was when she died that Noah began to fear nearly everything. First, he was afraid of losing his dad, too. Then he started to be afraid of random things, like taking the bus to school or falling down the stairs. Or setting the house on fire when cooking macaroni. At first, his fears were about people he loved getting hurt. But then he became fearful of even the smallest things.

It was why the grief counselor suggested he use a notebook, to write down everything he was afraid of. Noah was already twenty pages in.

But now Marvin had his notebook. And Noah wanted to write *shadow in the woods* down.

"Hey, Marvin," Noah called. Even with his long legs, Noah

had trouble keeping up with Marvin. Marvin was on a mission, chasing this mysterious figure. "Can I have my notebook back?"

But Marvin's head was clearly elsewhere.

"Did you see that guy?" Marvin asked both Noah and Tori. "He's real, right?"

Tori shrugged. "I'm not sure, I only saw a shadow."

The man in the old-timey prison clothes had looked like a real person, not a ghost.

"I saw him," Noah said. "But now he's gone." Noah wondered if Raven Island had the power to make you see ghosts somehow. If so, could see his mom again?

"And now here we are, wandering into the woods," Tori pointed out. "That's definitely going to get us some detention."

Noah couldn't help but notice that Tori seemed okay with that. She didn't seem afraid of anything. Noah was pretty sure that *getting detention* was one of his fears, written down somewhere on page two of his notebook.

As he looked around, Noah realized that Tori was right: they were well into the forest, the pine trees dense around them. The woodland path had gotten narrower, almost to the point that you were wondering if it was even there.

"But this path leads somewhere." Marvin was up ahead.

Tori and Marvin walked so fast that Noah had a hard time keeping up. While they walked at a leisurely pace, he was half running and out of breath.

"Man, it's cold here in the forest," Tori pointed out. The shade of the enormous pine trees made the temperature drop significantly.

Noah spotted a raven on one of the lower branches and then another one on the other side of the path. It was like the ravens were following the three of them. Boxing them in.

Marvin noticed them, too. "It's like that Hitchcock movie *The Birds*," he said.

Noah shook his head. "I've never seen it." But he sure had *raven* written in his notebook, inked in black pen just that morning when they were approaching Raven Island.

Marvin said, "My mom is into these old movies—*The Birds* is this classic Alfred Hitchcock movie."

"What's it about?" Tori asked.

"The birds go all bananas and attack people," Marvin said. "It's a creepy movie. Doesn't end well."

"Thanks for sharing, Marvin," Tori mumbled.

Noah could feel his worries building and also wished Marvin would keep quiet already. These ravens were creeping him out. He just kept thinking about this Edgar Allan Poe poem they'd read in class called "The Raven." "Nevermore," he mumbled to himself—it was what the raven kept saying in the poem. Now he was extra creeped out.

"Oh yeah," Marvin said. "Nevermore!" he called. But then he got a little creeped out, too—Noah could tell by the way Marvin's face fell.

"Let's get away from those birds," Tori said as she picked up the pace. Marvin and Noah did, too.

After about twenty minutes or so, they seemed to reach the end of the forest. And they were close to the edge of the island.

Noah could see the ocean, the choppy waters that went on forever. The Pacific always scared him. What was lurking under all that water?

"Look!" Marvin said, pointing to the far end of the island.

Noah followed Marvin's gaze. There were dark, billowing clouds, and the sky had a greenish tinge. The sun could barely peek through.

But up ahead, Noah saw what Marvin pointed to.

There it was: the Raven Island Lighthouse.

9
Friday, 1:16 p.m.

NOAH SAW THAT DARK CLOUDS WERE gathering overhead, like the universe was telling them:

Go away.

Then out of the corner of his eye, Noah saw a figure in prison stripes, rushing inside the lighthouse. "You see that?" he asked Tori and Marvin. "Someone just went inside."

"Let's go check it out," Marvin said.

Noah could tell that Marvin really wanted to make a run for it, but he slowed. So did Tori. Maybe they were chasing things just a little too easily here. That person could not be a nice guy.

Tori looked up at the lighthouse and the dark windows. "What if this dude is pulling us into some kind of trap?"

Noah was grateful that he wasn't the only one who was wondering if this was a good idea. He made a mental note to add *guy in prison costume* to his notebook, when he finally got it back from Marvin.

"You two are chickens," Marvin said with irritation in his voice. He charged ahead, while Noah and Tori hung back a little.

Then Tori groaned. "All right, all right. No one gets left behind—I guess that also applies when a person is going into a ghostly lighthouse by himself."

Noah had no choice but to follow, even though he felt a deep sense of dread. *Raven Island will take its bounty*—wasn't that what Mr. Thorne said?

Behind him, the trees seemed to huddle, closing in on each other. What if they never got to leave the island?

Noah forced himself to breathe and focus on the lighthouse up ahead.

The three of them braved the cold wind and made their way down the rocky path, toward the very tip of Raven Island. There was a raven flying overhead, wings spread as it looked down. At the three of them.

It was creeping Noah out, so he was grateful when they reached the door to get inside the lighthouse. Thankfully, it was unlocked. He had to push it open with both arms just so the wind wouldn't slam it shut.

The air inside was even colder than outside, which didn't seem possible, but it was definitely happening. Noah pulled at the zipper on his hoodie, but it was already all the way up. The lighthouse was extra quiet inside, especially now that they were out of the wind.

In front of them, there was a spiral staircase going up into the lighthouse. To the right, there was a stairway going down into a dark basement that Noah was only happy to ignore.

Noah was actually grateful when Marvin charged up the stairs—at least they weren't going down the other stairway.

He was last going up. He could hear his sneakers, squeaking as they hit the metal steps, up and up. And up some more.

Tori sighed above Noah. "I hate this place. It's like the whole island is designed to make the people on it miserable and lonely." Her voice echoed off the lighthouse's walls.

"It probably was," Noah said softly. "It's a prison."

"That doesn't make it right," Tori argued. "People just wanted the prisoners here locked up, so they could throw away the key and forget all about them."

Noah hadn't really thought about it that way, but Tori had a point.

They reached a landing with a giant window overlooking the island. Marvin rushed to look outside.

"You think the prisoners ever saw their families again?" Noah asked Tori.

But before she could answer, Marvin screamed, then covered his mouth. The sound echoed off the walls, and they both covered their ears.

"Sorry! You guys!" Marvin hissed from by the window. "You have to come quick!"

All three of them crowded by the dirty window. It was clouded over and covered in salt deposits, from all the ocean water that had sprayed it over the years.

"It's the dalgyal gwishin," Marvin whispered.

"What?" Noah asked.

"My grandma tells these old Korean ghost stories—anyway, just look," Marvin whispered.

From the tall window, they could see out over this cemetery. There was a big mausoleum, and all these tombstones.

But there also was a clearing, a spot where maybe they'd left room for another grave.

Only that empty space wasn't empty anymore. At the center, there were several men in striped uniforms, like the old kind. Noah remembered them from the movies he watched with his dad: they were light tan pants and button-up tops with black stripes. There were five prisoners, all digging in unison.

One of them was humming a tune. Noah knew it, from his mom's old records, but couldn't remember the name of the song.

He hummed it softly, along with the men down below.

There was no way those prisoners could've heard Noah, not way up there in the lighthouse, behind thick glass.

But they did. All five of them stopped digging. They turned their heads and looked up at the lighthouse.

Only the prisoners didn't have faces. No eyes, no nose, no mouth.

Just a black hole of nothing.

Right when Noah thought he might scream, he watched the faceless prisoners drop their shovels. They started walking.

Toward the lighthouse.

10
Friday, 1:30 p.m.

THEY RAN. TORI, NOAH, AND MARVIN went as fast as their sneakers would let them, rushing down the lighthouse stairs and out the door. Tori was terrified to run into those faceless prisoners. But she rushed outside anyway, along with Noah and Marvin.

Tori was afraid to even look toward the cemetery. She took the lead, since she was used to running from all that soccer practice. The gravel crunched under her feet. The air was freezing out here. It felt even colder than when they'd arrived at the lighthouse less than fifteen minutes ago.

Weren't cold spots a sign that ghosts were present?

She glanced back. Noah and Marvin ran together, looking terrified, too. But those prisoners, the ghosts?

They were gone.

Tori slowed her pace as she reached the edge of the forest. "You guys," she said, coming to a stop.

Marvin looked back. Noah was too afraid to at first, but then he looked toward the cemetery and the lighthouse as well.

"My grandma was right . . ." Marvin muttered. He added, "They're dalgyal gwishin—faceless ghosts. Well, technically, in Korean stories they're shaped more like an egg. My sisters used to scare me with old stories that my grandma would tell us . . ." Marvin shivered. "Dalgyal gwishin will show up in the forest, looking like a faceless egg shape. When you see them, you won't live long. They swallow you up. When I was little, my family liked to hike a lot. In the forest."

"Dude," Noah whispered. He looked terrified himself.

Tori tried not to look at the trees around them, but it was pretty hard.

Marvin added, "Dalgyal gwishin died without loved ones to remember them. That's why they're faceless. Just like those ghosts in the graveyard."

Those faceless ghosts scared the heck out of Tori. "Let's go," she said, motioning toward the forest path.

Noah pulled Marvin's arm. "We can't miss the ferry, remember?"

Tori was already walking into the forest. This place scared her. She wanted to get to the dock already.

"Yeah, all right," Marvin muttered, but you could tell he really wanted to stick around the island, despite the dalgyal gwishin.

They had been walking for a while when Tori began to wonder why they weren't at the prison yet.

"I don't remember the path being this narrow," Noah said with a tremor in his voice.

"I'm sure we'll get to the prison any minute now," Tori said, to keep Noah and Marvin calm. "These trees look familiar," she added, but she really wasn't sure herself. Tori was forging ahead, even though the pine branches were hitting her in the legs and her shoulders and trying to slow her down.

Marvin slowed. "I think Noah may be right. The path was narrow, but not *this* narrow. And I don't remember seeing a creek." He pointed between the pines to a creek that tumbled down some stones.

"There's a clearing up ahead," Noah pointed out. "Maybe we'll just come out at a different part."

But Tori was starting to realize that this was all wrong. It was like when she was standing in the goal, looking out on the field. She could see the big picture, the way none of the other players seemed to be able to. Tori felt her stomach sink.

They weren't headed back the way they came after all.

But before Tori could go into full-blown panic mode, a man seemed to appear out of nowhere. "Children—on Raven Island?" The man was short, Hispanic, had a trimmed beard, and was wearing a black suit of some sort. It was the same kind Mr. Thorne wore. Was he a tour guide like Mr. Thorne? Tori wondered. The man asked, "What are you doing here?"

"We're trying to find our way back to the prison so that we can get on the ferry," Tori said, doing her best to hide her worry and irritation. "Can you help?"

"Of course." The man smiled. He seemed very friendly, even though they had no idea who he was. And they were in a creepy forest. On a ghostly island.

But Tori figured they didn't have too much of a choice, so she followed him, along with Marvin and Noah.

And in no time at all, they were back at the prison.

"Thanks," Tori said. The other students were already moving along to get to the dock.

"De nada," the man said, and then he . . .

Disappeared.

Before Tori could say anything, Noah and Marvin froze.

"Dude!" Marvin whispered. "That guy was definitely a ghost."

"We don't know that," Tori said, but she knew she was lying. That man was indeed a ghost.

"At least he was helpful," Noah said, and shrugged.

All three kids broke out laughing. It felt good—Tori hadn't laughed in what felt like forever.

"We need to catch the ferry," Tori said as they walked to the overlook, and she saw the rest of their grade boarding the boat.

It was two o'clock.

Time to go.

11
Friday, 2:09 p.m.

MARVIN'S HEAD WAS SPINNING WHEN HE got in line for roll call. He'd seen a ghost—scratch that, several ghosts! Sure, he'd also run like the wind once he saw them, but that was beside the point.

There were ghosts, right here on Raven Island! If he'd had his phone, he could've recorded the whole thing for this movie . . .

"Remember, no phones until we're all on the ferry," Mr. Thompson said. He sounded tired and ready to go home.

Tori and Noah stood around near Marvin, on the lower deck. They were some of the last ones to get on.

Marvin bounced on his heels. He had an idea. It was a bad one, probably, but a good one if you looked at it the right way. At least Marvin thought so.

He watched Mr. Thompson close his tablet and get on the ferry. There was the metal chain that the teacher clipped to the ferry's wall. Like the kind they have at amusement parks, to make you wait your turn.

Marvin looked out on the water, at the tiny strip of sandy beach that wrapped around the island on the north side. There was a rowboat with oars inside, moored on the sand.

Suddenly, there was a man. It was that same guy who had

helped them out of the woods—the prison guard. The man was putting the oars into the boat.

And there were three other men, a very tall bald one with a menacing look in his dark eyes and two shorter guys with blond hair who looked alike. All three men were wearing prison stripes. The men had startled the tour guide who had helped them find their way back to the prison. The tall bald prisoner grabbed one of the oars.

They had a conversation—or rather, an argument. The tour guide kept shaking his head.

"Are you all seeing this?" Marvin asked. Tori and Noah nodded, both looking scared. The rest of the class was already inside, too busy talking to each other to look back at the island.

And just as quickly as the tour guide and the prisoners appeared, they had disappeared. So did the boat. Only one prisoner still stood there: this tall, older guy with a shaved head, wearing prison stripes. He stalked off, back toward the prison and out of sight.

Marvin felt a chill go down his spine, like someone dropped an ice cube down the back of his shirt. Were those people ghosts?

"What *was* that?" Tori asked in a shaky voice.

"That was the guard ghost!" Noah said. "And those prisoners are ghosts, too—all three of them!"

Marvin nodded. "They're mul gwishin—ghosts of people who drowned." His sisters would be scared if they saw what he'd just seen. Maybe he could tell them all about it once he got home.

"Like the dalgyal gwishin," Noah said. "Only in the water."

Marvin nodded. He shivered as he remembered the nightmares he'd had when he was little, of mul gwishin crawling from the water, their skin pale, their arms like stretching tentacles. Not that these ghosts looked like that, exactly. But still! He couldn't leave Raven Island now, not when there were ghostly appearances right in front of him!

The ferry horn blew.

Marvin felt a familiar buzz inside his head. It was the kind he got when he was about to do something against the rules.

"That was really creepy," Tori muttered next to him. "I'm glad we're outta here."

Mr. Thompson went inside the ferry cabin rather than staying on the dock. There was a drizzle, and just about all the kids huddled inside the ferry.

And right before the ferry started to move, Marvin took a step over the chain.

"Yo, Marvin, what are you doing?" Noah asked behind him.

But Marvin ignored him. He hopped off the ferry and started walking up the path toward the prison.

"Marvin!" Tori hissed behind him.

He kept going. Marvin had a plan. He was going to spend the night on Raven Island and make his movie. Catch all these ghosts on video with his phone.

Only, then Noah came after him. And Tori, too.

"We have to go back, Marvin!" Tori said. The ferry was already pulling away. The only way they could get back on was if they jumped.

Maybe.

But Marvin was determined: he was *not* getting back on that ferry.

No matter what.

11
Trapped on Raven Island

12

Friday, 2:25 p.m.

NOAH FELT PANIC SPREAD ACROSS HIS chest as he watched the ferry pull away from the docks. He tried waving both his arms over his head.

He yelled, "Stop!"

And Tori did, too. But the kids, teacher, and chaperones were all inside rather than standing on the ferry deck, so they wouldn't be able to see them anyway. Everyone had their buddy, so no one would miss them. Until it was too late, and they were already back to shore.

Noah had to force himself to breathe. Being stuck on Raven Island was definitely at the very, *very* top of the list of things he was afraid of. What if they couldn't get home tonight?

"We'll be here all night now," Tori said next to him, her arms limp at her sides.

"But that's kinda cool. Right?" Marvin said.

Both Tori and Noah turned to Marvin. And Noah was afraid of Tori now, and afraid for Marvin for being at the receiving end of her wrath.

Tori's hands turned to fists at her side. "No, Marvin, that's *not* cool. At all. Some of us would prefer to be home tonight, in our own beds. Not stuck on a haunted island."

"Yeah," Noah muttered. Thinking of the ghosts he'd seen made him feel like throwing up. Because that was during the day. Imagine what Raven Island was like at night . . .

"Just think about the ghosts that will be coming out when it gets dark!" Marvin said with a smile, like he was reading Noah's mind.

Tori shook her head and stalked off. "I'm going to see if there's a way to contact the grown-ups. Maybe there's a phone at the prison. You want to come, Noah?"

Noah nodded and followed. But he did feel like he owed Marvin, for standing up for him against Liam.

Marvin followed, too, but he trailed behind. He was all too happy to be stuck on Raven Island. He was the one who'd jumped off the ferry, after all.

Noah felt his heart bang against his rib cage. Surely Mr. Thompson would realize they were missing. Right? The teacher was supposed to be his buddy, after all.

But Noah knew that sometimes things don't work out the way you want them to. Sometimes really bad things happen. Like losing your mom forever. Even if you're barely twelve years old, and you don't suspect it can happen to you.

They'd reached the prison and went inside through the double doors. To Noah, it seemed like it was already getting darker . . . Tori stalked ahead of him toward the dome in the center, to the guards' station where the *Ghost Catchers* crew had set up their computer.

The prison was slowly turning into a film set around them.

This short, lighter-skinned Black woman with a pixie cut, dressed in dark clothing, was holding a clipboard. That was promising, Noah thought. People with clipboards had plans, they were doers. And the three of them needed someone like that to help them get off Raven Island. Or at least, to find a phone.

"Excuse me?" Noah asked. He tapped the lady on her shoulder.

She spun around, looking startled. "Oh, kid—don't ever do that again! You know I'm looking for ghosts, right?"

"Right. Sorry for startling you, but we need help." Noah heard Marvin shift behind him. And Tori felt like a giant thundercloud.

The woman squinted. "Wait—weren't you kids part of that tour group? And aren't you supposed to be on the ferry that just left?"

The conversation caught the attention of Tammy, the prankster who rang the death bell during the tour. She made her way over. "What's going on, Sarah?"

"We've got stowaways, Tam," Sarah said, nodding toward the three of them.

"Technically, we're more like stragglers," Marvin said. "Since we're not on a boat."

Tammy grinned. "Well, I hope you brought your toothbrushes, kids, because you're stuck here for the night."

"I know!" Marvin said, all excited. "We already saw a bunch of ghosts—at the cemetery, and by the docks."

"Hmmm," Sarah said. "Maybe we could use you kids."

"No, you won't," Tori argued. "We're getting out of here. I'm sure they can send someone to come get us. Right?"

Sarah and Tammy laughed. *This is not a good sign,* Noah thought.

Noah couldn't believe how calm they were about the fact that three kids were still on Raven Island. But then he remembered: the important thing was that they called home. His dad was going to flip. "We need a phone."

Tammy said, "The only phones here are the former inmate ones, and they have been out of commission since the prison shut down."

Sarah thumbed over her shoulder toward the other side of Raven Island. "You'll want to make your way to the mansion. Ms. Chavez has a working landline."

"You think the mansion is haunted?" Marvin asked, sounding way too excited.

"Who cares?" Tori said. "We just need to call home." Tori was already walking away, and Noah could see Marvin hesitate. But then he followed Tori.

"Thanks," Noah said to Sarah. He was about to join his friends when Sarah pulled his sleeve.

"Hey, kid," she said softly.

"It's Noah. My name is Noah," he responded.

Sarah nodded. "Noah. Be careful out there. This island is full of . . . unexpected residents."

"Ghosts, you mean," Noah said. "Like I said, we met a few of them."

Sarah hesitated. "Not just ghosts. There are . . . unexpected residents, and—"

"Noah, come on!" Tori called, almost at the tree line already. Marvin had his phone out and seemed to be filming.

"I'm coming!" Noah called.

He turned back to Sarah, but all he saw was a closing door.

Noah went to join Marvin and Tori, but he felt a nagging dread in his gut.

Unexpected residents.

That sure sounded like bad news.

13
Friday, 3:15 p.m.

MARVIN COULD BARELY CONTAIN HIS EXCITEMENT. They were stuck on Raven Island! He actually pulled it off—though he felt kind of bad about dragging Tori and Noah along. But then again, they didn't have to follow him; that was their own choice . . . right?

He'd make it up to them.

Marvin followed along as Tori and Noah tried to find a phone. He figured it would be a good idea to let his mom and dad know what happened anyway. He didn't want them to freak out when he didn't come home from school.

Marvin felt bad for breaking all these rules and worrying everyone, but only a little. As they walked out of the prison, he was already planning out the shots he'd take for his movie. He was lucky to have a great phone that allowed him to shoot in high definition, and it even had an editing app that made it easy to make a very professional-looking movie. He could shoot a scene with the pine trees looming overhead, or up close with a flashlight in someone's face . . .

He was going to make his movie about the prison escape. Marvin felt his ideas coming together already. And maybe this mansion was haunted . . .

The rain had stopped, but the wind was picking up now, giving the three of them no break from the elements. Marvin could feel the cold air blow right through his clothes.

Marvin charged ahead of Tori and Noah. The sooner they called home, the sooner he could get to filming his movie. He guessed that once it got dark, the ghosts would be coming out from every corner. And once Tori and Noah got over the fact that they were stuck on the island, maybe they'd help him with his movie. But Marvin knew it wasn't quite time to reveal his motives for ditching the ferry ride.

Noah rushed to catch up with Marvin. The pine trees were swaying in the wind, making this creepy howling sound.

Noah ran-jogged to catch up. He asked, "Do you think they'll send a boat to come get us?"

"They can't," Marvin answered. "That current is for real, Noah."

"Right." Noah bit his lip. "How about a helicopter?" His voice was squeaky, and he looked terrified.

Tori laughed bitterly behind them. "Those cost, like, thousands of dollars to dispatch. We're stuck here!"

Noah stepped back. "Right. Yeah."

Marvin leaned closer to Noah. "Don't let her bad attitude bring you down."

"What are you talking about?" Tori said, pushing herself to walk between them.

Marvin had to watch out or the pine tree branches would smack him in the head. He said, "You've been ready to punch anyone who comes near you since . . . Well, for months now."

Tori looked at him. "Are you spying on me, Marv?"

Marvin flustered.

"It's not like you could miss it," Noah said, his voice trailing. "Not that it's my business."

At first, Tori seemed to get angrier, but then her face softened. "You're right. I've been dealing with some stuff and—"

Out of nowhere, a pine branch smacked Tori in the head.

"What was that?" Marvin asked.

Noah whispered, "Was that a ghost?"

Tori jumped. "That's it! Let's go find this mansion and get out of here." She rushed ahead and Noah followed.

Marvin looked at the tree one more time, but it just stood there, swaying in the cold breeze.

Maybe it was just the wind.

And maybe the forest was haunted! Marvin had to make sure he came to film in the woods. Tonight. What if the trees were alive . . . ? What if the island wouldn't let them leave . . . ?

That idea made Marvin downright scared.

Marvin turned and hurried to join Tori and Noah. They were now reaching the end of the forest, right near the owner's mansion. It was dark, because a storm was coming.

The mansion was wide and square, built out of the same stone as the prison. Overgrown vines crawled up the walls, like they were trying to swallow the building. A large circular driveway looped in front, as if cars could pull right up to drop guests for a fancy dinner party. Only there were no cars. And the only guests were ghosts, and a few straggler kids.

There were large double doors at the center of the mansion, with a flickering chandelier under a small overhang.

Tori stopped. "Do we just ring the doorbell?"

Marvin looked at the mansion. In the dark light of the stormy weather, the place looked foreboding. The brick was crumbling; you could even see that from afar.

Lightning struck. Marvin jumped, but he also couldn't help but see lots of opportunity for his movie's storyboard. Flashes of lightning could illuminate a ghost but then leave his main characters in darkness after . . . That would be cool.

"Is anyone even home?" Noah asked next to him.

Marvin pointed to the side of the mansion, where dim light shone from one of the main-floor windows. "There—someone's here."

"Let's go," Tori said.

But before Marvin could move, he felt an icy gust of wind down his neck.

And someone yelled in his ear: "What are you scoundrels doing here?"

14
Friday, 3:45 p.m.

TORI FELT A COLD SWIRL OF air surround them. She instinctively pulled back, but couldn't get away. There was a waft of cigarette smoke that wrapped around her like a stinky blanket.

"You!" Mr. Thorne, who had given them the tour of the prison earlier that day, looked like he wanted to kill her with his dark, laser-focused eyes. His pale face was in a scowl, and he crossed his arms.

Noah called, "Let them go!" But he stepped back himself.

Way to be brave, Noah, Tori thought. But she couldn't really get mad at him. This caretaker was vicious as an attack dog.

"Why aren't you on the ferry?" Mr. Thorne's breath smelled like stale coffee. His skin was pasty, like maybe he was sick.

Tori pulled as far away from the man as she could. "We missed it," she said, even though that was far from the whole truth.

"We saw a bunch of ghosts at the cemetery!" Marvin said, also doing his best to pull away from Mr. Thorne. "And at the docks."

That got his attention. Mr. Thorne let go of their sleeves and frowned. "Ghosts?"

"Yes." Tori adjusted her shirt. "There was this man dressed in an old prison outfit. He disappeared into the woods, and then when we followed him, we found these ghosts at the cemetery."

"They were dead. *Very* dead," Noah added, like there were varying degrees of deadness.

Then Marvin told Mr. Thorne about the prisoners and the tour guide ghost they saw at the docks.

Mr. Thorne grumbled. "We need to talk to Ms. Chavez about all this. Come with me."

Tori followed, and Noah and Marvin caught up quickly.

"Do you think they can send a boat to come get us?" Noah asked with hope in his voice.

Mr. Thorne let out a sarcastic laugh, which turned into a rolling smoker's cough.

"I'll take that as a no on the boat rescue," Marvin whispered next to her. Of course, Tori knew that Marvin was completely fine with that.

"Thank you, Marvin."

Tori rushed ahead toward the mansion's double doors. She stuffed her hands into her pockets, clasping the stress ball with all the force she could muster. Tori could barely contain her anger. They were honestly stuck here on this cold, wet, and creepy island.

Instead of walking to the double doors in front, Mr. Thorne took a hard right, around the mansion. "We go in through the kitchen, out back."

Tori tried her best to walk off her anger. She had to hurry

to catch up to Mr. Thorne, who was surprisingly fast for not exactly being a tall guy. As Tori turned the corner of the mansion, she felt a tug at her sleeve. Something grabbed her, wrapping its fingers or tentacles around her arm.

"*Aarghhh!*" she called, and jumped. One of the mansion's vines had hit her again.

"Dude, that vine was trying to grab you," Marvin whispered.

"Maybe the mansion doesn't want you to leave," Noah said.

A gust of wind blew around the kids, and Tori shivered.

"Children!" Mr. Thorne called from the door at the back. "Let's go inside."

Tori wanted to keep moving. The mansion smelled musty, and faintly of some kind of cake. It reminded her how hungry she was.

They followed Mr. Thorne through the kitchen, which was huge but old and worn. The cabinets looked dingy and were missing doors here and there. The stove was probably an antique by now, and the windows were so dirty they cast a gray glow over the room.

But there was a cake on a cooling rack. Tori's mouth watered.

"This way," Mr. Thorne called ahead of her. They went through another set of double doors, down a hallway, and into a sitting room. Four large leather chairs surrounded an enormous stone fireplace that had logs but no fire. The room was freezing. And Ms. Chavez sat in one of the chairs, reading a book.

"What is this?" Ms. Chavez put down her book and stood.

"We missed the ferry," Tori said. She once again left out the part where Marvin jumped off and they followed.

Ms. Chavez frowned, but didn't seem particularly upset. "How is this possible? I spoke to your teacher, and he assured me you would all leave promptly at two."

Mr. Thorne said nothing.

"I should've seen you off myself," Ms. Chavez muttered.

"Do you have, like, an extra boat?" Noah asked. He stepped forward. "Or a helicopter?"

Ms. Chavez smiled like the whole thing was very entertaining. "I may own the island, but I don't own the elements."

Noah looked at her like he was still expecting something.

Ms. Chavez said, "The ocean currents won't allow any vessel to travel until tomorrow, I'm afraid. Plus, the air vortices are just as lethal. And I don't have a helicopter, young man."

"So we're stuck here?" Noah's voice had a tremor to it.

Ms. Chavez sighed. "I'm afraid so. You can call home using the phone in the sitting room."

Tori was about to go find this sitting room when she remembered something.

"Ms. Chavez," she said. "You should probably know that there are ghosts, all over the island." Tori told Ms. Chavez about the ghosts at the cemetery, about the ghost man who led them back to the prison, and then the three prisoner and tour-guide ghosts they saw at the docks.

Ms. Chavez's face went even paler than it already was. "At the docks?"

There was a silence, then Ms. Chavez let out a breath. "So it is true: children can see ghosts when adults can't."

Tori couldn't believe her ears. "Wait—you can't see them?"

Ms. Chavez shook her head with a sad smile. "Not so far. There's anecdotal evidence that kids have a way of seeing the spirit world. Will you tell me next time you see a spirit?"

Tori nodded.

But she was really hoping she would make it through the night without seeing another ghost . . . And Tori suddenly had a deep sense that she was in danger. That the three of them were.

There was a long night ahead of them. A night of ghosts, danger, and an island determined to hold on to its secrets.

Tori couldn't wait for daybreak to come.

15
Friday, 4:01 p.m.

"WHO WANTS TO CALL HOME FIRST?" Ms. Chavez asked, stirring Tori from her thoughts.

The conversation had drifted away from their ghost encounters, with Ms. Chavez looking like she had lots on her mind. And like she had secrets. But Tori knew it was time to call home and let her mom know she was spending the night on Raven Island.

Tori still couldn't believe it. Part of her wished she'd just left Marvin behind. But then a bigger part of her knew that wasn't the right thing to do. She may not be the goalie right now, but being part of a team her whole life instilled the belief in Tori that no one should be left behind.

"I'll go first," she said. Tori wasn't looking forward to this call.

Tori followed Ms. Chavez back to the sitting room, where there was a small table with an old rotary phone on it.

"I'll leave you to it," Ms. Chavez said before walking away.

She had to concentrate to remember her mom's cell phone number—all her contacts were programmed into her phone, which was in her backpack (and probably down to very little battery).

Her mom's phone rang and rang, but she didn't pick up. Looking at the clock, Tori realized her mom would be waiting for her to get off the bus right that very minute.

After the beep, she left her message.

"Hi, Mom. I'll bet you're waiting for me to get off the bus right now. The thing is, I missed the ferry, along with a couple of other kids."

She swallowed, and suddenly she felt like crying.

"But I don't want you to worry about me." She knew how much her mom lost sleep about Danny, about him being in jail, and about his safety. Last thing her mom needed was more concerns.

Tori swallowed her tears away. "I'm fine, and the lady who owns the island is really nice." She wasn't entirely sure about that, but she said so for her mom's peace of mind. "I'll catch the ferry in the morning. You won't even know I'm gone. Love you."

The beep of the voicemail cut off her last words. Tori sighed, and put the phone on the receiver.

"She's not that nice, you know," Mr. Thorne said, making her jump.

Tori jumped up. "Mr. Thorne! Stop sneaking up on people." Now she felt that anger flare up again. "You're creeping everyone out."

She rushed past him to the giant room with the fireplace where Noah and Marvin were waiting. Ms. Chavez had disappeared.

"Tori," Marvin said, lighting up.

"Yeah." She forced herself to smile and not think of her mom, standing there waiting for her to get off the bus.

Then she realized that Marvin and Noah had been talking

while she was gone. They'd been hatching a plan—she could see it in their eyes.

Noah sat up. "We have an idea. Something to do while we're waiting for tomorrow's ferry."

Marvin continued, "You know how we saw those prisoners and the tour guide. Right?"

Tori nodded, unsure where this was going.

"We have a plan," Marvin said. "We're going to figure out what happened to those escaped prisoners."

16
Friday, 4:20 p.m.

MARVIN THOUGHT TORI LOOKED A LITTLE off. Sad, and more so than you'd expect. He knew she wasn't excited about being stuck on the island. Even if Marvin was.

But Noah wasn't picking up on Tori's mood. "We're going to collect evidence, like it's a detective case," he said in a half whisper. "Find out what happened to the escaped prisoners and try to figure out whether they're alive or not." Noah still looked nervous, but excited, too. Marvin was glad he was coming around.

The room felt cold and deserted to Marvin. He was ready to keep moving already, and get out of this creepy mansion.

Noah added, "And then we're going to help Marvin make his movie."

"Look, I'm all for solving the mystery of this prison escape," Tori said. "But I'm not helping Marvin with his movie. He's the reason we're stuck here in the first place!"

"And I'm sorry about that," Marvin said, even if he wasn't. "But you have to admit: this is the perfect opportunity. Think of all the ghosts we'll see!"

Noah said, "They say the spirits of the dead can't leave. The ones with unfinished business are stuck haunting Raven Island forever."

Tori muttered, "These poor ghost prisoners, stuck on Raven Island for decades . . ."

Marvin said, "Maybe we can help put them to rest."

Tori seemed to think about that for a long moment, but then she nodded. "Okay, I'm in. Let's help the dead prisoners find peace."

"You think we could see other ghosts?" Noah asked. "Like, ones that didn't die here?"

Tori shrugged. "Seems like Raven Island is full of ghosts, but who knows? Anyway, what's the plan?"

Marvin said, "We don't know yet. Not exactly." He was about to add that they should brainstorm ideas when he felt the hair on the back of his neck stand up.

Marvin turned around, only to look right into two bright white eyes set in a dark brown face. "*Arrrghhh!*" he yelped. And when he composed himself, he asked, "Who are you?"

"I'm Beatrice. Bea." Her voice was like a whisper. She pulled at her long braid. "I'm the bird keeper."

"Nice to meet you," Noah said with a smile. He was the friendliest guy. He even extended his hand to shake Bea's, but she just looked at it like it was radioactive.

Tori said, "You take care of those ravens?"

Bea nodded and smiled.

"Children," Mr. Thorne called from the hallway. "It's time for dinner."

—

Marvin waited for Noah to call home. He also looked kind of

sad afterward. Then it was Marvin's turn. His mom actually sounded like she was crying.

Marvin couldn't remember the last time he'd missed dinner. Probably when he was away at filmmaking camp last year. Dinner was a big deal at his house: either his grandma or mom and sometimes his dad would cook a full meal, or work with the previous day's leftovers to make bibimbap. His sisters would be talking over each other, his dad would have some good stories from the restaurant—Marvin could barely get a word in most days. But hearing his mom's voice, he felt a pang of homesickness.

"I'm fine, Mom. The people here are really nice." Okay, so maybe that was a little bit of a lie. They were mostly very creepy, but he wasn't about to tell his mom that. "I'll be on the ferry at daybreak."

His mom reluctantly agreed and told him to call before he got on the ferry.

Marvin said he would. He was still thinking of dinner at home when he made it to the dining room, where everyone was seated around an enormous wooden table. It was a funny scene: Noah and Tori looking tired and irritated; Mr. Thorne, who didn't even have a plate; quiet Bea, who didn't seem to blink; and Ms. Chavez, who tried to smile.

As Marvin slid into the seat next to Tori, he thought about his movie. He could call it *Death on Raven Island.*

No, he needed a better title. But he was feeling that familiar fire in his gut. Now he just had to get his head into the moviemaking game.

Marvin looked down at his bowl. It was tomato soup, his least favorite kind. Sure not his dad's bibimbap.

"I'm afraid dinner is somewhat of a compromise," Ms. Chavez said from the head of the table.

"I like soup," Noah said. "My dad and I eat soup at least twice a week."

"Dude, that's sad," Marvin said before he could think about it.

"There's nothing wrong with soup," Tori said. She slurped a big spoonful to demonstrate.

"Didn't know you were the soup police," Marvin mumbled. But he did feel a little bad. He was spoiled, with a chef for a mom and his grandma's Korean cooking. But Noah probably didn't have that.

"Enough with the arguing," Ms. Chavez said. "Bon appétit." She passed the bread to Bea, who took a slice. "Why aren't you eating, Mr. Thorne?" she asked.

Mr. Thorne shook his head. "I'm not hungry, thank you."

Ms. Chavez frowned, but then asked, "Did you kids enjoy the tour?"

Noah nodded.

Tori was silent. For some reason, she really hated that prison. Marvin couldn't figure out why.

Marvin said, "It was interesting. Is it really true that more than two thousand people died on the island?"

"Yes," Ms. Chavez answered.

"And so many are buried in that graveyard, right?" Marvin said, more of a statement than a question. He wanted to learn more about the dead on the island. Maybe then they could figure out the story behind those faceless gravediggers—the dalgyal gwishin his sisters used to scare him with—that they'd seen at the cemetery.

"The sanatorium dug some mass graves," Ms. Chavez said. "And then there were the prisoners who died while building the prison. It is unknown how many dead are on the island."

"Can we stop talking about dead people, please?" Tori said, her voice raised. "I'm trying to enjoy my soup."

"Yum," Noah said softly. He was attempting to be a peacemaker.

But Marvin wasn't going to be silenced. This was his opportunity to get information from Ms. Chavez, for his movie. "So your dad was a warden here?" he asked her, trying to sound casual.

She just nodded. Ms. Chavez finished her soup and set her bowl aside. "For a few months. I even lived right here in this house. In the room you'll be sleeping in."

Marvin made a face. He couldn't imagine someone actually living in this mansion. Also, he was just reminded that they would be spending the night here. But there was no way he was sleeping—he had a movie to make.

"You actually lived on the island?" Noah asked. "Were there other kids?"

Ms. Chavez shook her head. "Just me. The warden was expected to live here in the mansion with his family. Most days, it was just me and my mother." She looked sad. "In the beginning, it was an adventure: this house, the grounds, the forest. But I got bored, so I went exploring. To the prison."

"Didn't your parents get mad at you?" Marvin asked. His

mother and father wouldn't let him leave the house if they lived on a prison island, he knew that for sure.

Ms. Chavez shrugged. "They were different times, perhaps. And my mother was busy getting this mansion settled. I would follow my father to the prison. He didn't know." She smiled. "I was quite the troublemaker."

Marvin could relate.

"But I felt the island sometimes," Ms. Chavez said. She took a piece of bread and pulled it into small pieces. "Like it was a living being. Sometimes I would spend what felt like minutes in the forest, but I would be gone for hours. And the prison . . . Well, you've been there."

"What was it like when it was still operational?" Marvin asked. He was thinking of his movie and gathering story ideas.

"Cold," Ms. Chavez said. "Quiet—too quiet. Like the men inside were already dead."

Marvin swallowed.

Ms. Chavez continued, "I even met some of the prisoners."

"Were any of them in cell fourteen?" Noah asked. "They say it's cursed."

"It is," Mr. Thorne said.

Tori cleared her throat and shifted in her seat. She looked like she was ready to blow up.

"Yes," Ms. Chavez said with a nod. "I met the last prisoner to die in cell fourteen."

17
Friday, 5:35 p.m.

MARVIN HELD HIS BREATH, WAITING FOR Ms. Chavez to tell her story. You could hear a pin drop in the dining room. Bea let out a tiny chirp, like a bird.

"There was a prisoner named Joseph Fink," Ms. Chavez continued. She tore her bread into small pieces but didn't eat any of it. "He was a vicious killer, with several murders on his record. When he came to Raven Island, all the guards were afraid of him. Even the other prisoners."

"But not the birds," Bea said in her whisper-thin voice. "The birds loved him."

Ms. Chavez nodded. "Mr. Fink was first placed in the fourth wing, which was unoccupied other than his cell. But his silence made everyone more afraid. So they put him in cell fourteen, hoping the prison would take care of him."

"Did it kill him?" Marvin asked. He'd been holding his breath, imagining Mr. Fink as a large giant of a man, in the dark behind the long shadows of the prison bars. He could practically see it, like a movie.

"Not at first," Ms. Chavez answered. "In fact, he lived for months in cell fourteen. He was so quiet, the birds started visiting him through the tiny slit of a window."

"Finches," Bea said, nodding. "The small birds liked him the most."

"They called him the Birdman. He would whistle this tune—'Danse Macabre,' a creepy composition if you've ever heard it—and they'd hop right up to the window." Ms. Chavez smiled, but it was a sad smile, like she remembered something bad. "When we first moved to Raven Island, I wasn't happy. I missed my friends, and I was running from the mansion. I roamed, unbeknownst to my parents, until I reached the window of cell fourteen. Of course, I didn't know it was cell fourteen at the time. I just saw a window. And I saw the birds."

No one spoke. Marvin held his breath, afraid he would make too much noise.

"That was the first and only time that Mr. Fink and I met," Ms. Chavez said. Her eyes darkened. "He whistled a tune to the birds and fed them tiny bits of bread. As a little girl, I was fascinated by all animals. On Raven Island, they were my only friends. So I sat there outside that prison cell and watched him. We never spoke, but so much was said anyway."

Everyone looked at their bread. Suddenly, Marvin wasn't hungry anymore.

"He died the next day," Ms. Chavez said, exhaling the words.

"How did he die?" Marvin asked.

Ms. Chavez gave the tiniest of shrugs. "In his sleep. Perhaps a heart attack, perhaps from just the sheer sadness of the prison. There was no foul play, from what my father could gather. Mr. Fink, like all the prisoners on Raven Island, was disposed of, forgotten by those on the mainland. I went to see him that day, but the birds had already left. It was the loneliest feeling."

Ms. Chavez said softly, "There was no one to claim his body. He was buried at the Raven Island cemetery."

That was unbelievably sad. Marvin found it hard to breathe. Next to him, Tori shifted in her seat again. She seemed angry, though Marvin couldn't figure out why.

"I came here to make a difference, like my father," Ms. Chavez said.

Tori huffed.

Marvin asked, "Is Mr. Fink haunting Raven Island?"

Ms. Chavez looked unsure.

But then the caretaker's gravelly voice went, "You can hear the Birdman whistle in the small hours of the morning."

Tori pushed her chair back loudly and stood. "Excuse me."

And she rushed out of the dining room.

18
Friday, 6:09 p.m.

TORI HAD TO FORCE HERSELF TO breathe. She leaned against the closest wall. The thought of that prison and the forgotten men inside made her think of her brother.

Was he locked up like that right now, with only a tiny window to look out onto the world? Did he think that everyone had forgotten him? Did he think *she* had forgotten him?

Plus, there was Ms. Chavez, talking about that friendship with the Birdman like she was so nice. But what about her father, the last warden of Raven Island Prison? Wasn't he responsible for the treatment of these men? And their deaths, too?

Tori hated Raven Island, and she hated Ms. Chavez.

She was so angry, she couldn't get her breathing under control. She continued to gasp for air and rushed down another hallway. There were doors on either side—she just wanted to leave.

She fumbled and tried a door to her right. It opened, making the smallest popping sound of air unlocking, like opening up a jar of jam.

Tori hurried inside, closed the door behind her, and leaned against it. Her anger was slowly fading, making way for a familiar sadness and loneliness.

Tori turned on the light and looked around. She was in an

office with wood paneling, another stone fireplace (understandably, since the mansion was like a freezer), and oil paintings on the wall. Each was of some older guy—the wardens of the prison, Tori guessed.

Over the fireplace was a painting of the only man who wasn't white: a Hispanic man with darker skin and black hair, short, looking off in the distance with a pained look in his eyes. This had to be Mr. Chavez, the last warden of Raven Island's prison. No wonder he looked so miserable.

And Tori realized she recognized him.

This was the man who had helped them out of the forest and back to the prison!

And he was the ghost on the beach—only, he wasn't a prison guard. Mr. Chavez was the warden. But why was his ghost talking to those prisoners on the beach? Wasn't he basically the boss of Raven Island?

None of what they saw made sense.

There was a heavy wooden desk with a wall of bookcases behind it. Tori walked up to it and sat down in the chair.

So this was where the warden had controlled the fate of all those men who the world had already forgotten, deciding whether to lock them in solitary confinement or grant them the chance at parole.

Tori felt a knot in her chest and anger bubbling just below that knot. She had to pull it together. They were stuck here on Raven Island until tomorrow's ferry—that was still a good twelve hours away. She couldn't be losing her cool every time someone talked about dead prisoners.

But it was impossible not to think of her brother. Tori clenched her jaw, and she banged the desk with her fist. It felt good to let that bottled-up anger out, so she hit it again.

And again. Harder that time.

There was a crack and then a thud. Something had fallen under the desk and landed by her feet.

Tori pulled the chair out from behind the desk and bent down to get a closer look. There, on the expensive-looking rug, was a dusty black notebook.

She crawled under the desk and picked up the book. Tori sat on the rug, crouched under the desk, and looked up. There was a compartment that had opened, probably because she hit the desk so hard.

A secret compartment.

Tori opened the notebook. *January 2, 1972.* Then someone had written, in hard-to-read cursive, for pages and pages.

This was a journal. She looked at the inside cover of the notebook.

Fernando Chavez. The last warden of Raven Island Prison.

"Tori?" Noah called, and opened the door.

Tori looked up and bumped her head on the desk. "Ouch! Yeah, I'm in here."

"Dude, what is this place?" she heard Marvin ask behind Noah. "Like, someone's office?"

She tucked the notebook in her waistband and crawled out from under the desk. "The warden's office," Tori said as she stood up and pushed the chair back.

Noah whispered, "We need to get out of here, before Ms. Chavez finds us."

There was a waft of cigarette smoke, and Tori froze.

"That seems like an excellent idea," Mr. Thorne said behind the two boys.

Busted, Tori thought.

"Out, right now," Mr. Thorne grumbled. "It's about time I locked you brats in for the night."

19

Friday, 6:51 p.m.

"LET'S GO." MR. THORNE MADE THEM walk ahead, down the hall and up a rickety set of narrow stairs off the kitchen. "First door on the right."

Noah kept moving forward, but that caretaker was really giving him the creeps.

"Where are you taking us?" Tori asked once they reached the second floor.

Marvin added, "Yeah, and where is Ms. Chavez?"

"She has an emergency to attend to," Mr. Thorne said, ushering them toward the open door to the right. "Now, get inside."

"What kind of emergency?" Noah asked.

But Mr. Thorne didn't answer.

The room was large and had four beds and four matching dressers. There was a dusty overhead light. And a door that led to a bathroom.

"There are blankets and sheets inside each of the dressers," Mr. Thorne said. "And some nightgowns and pajamas." He still stood in the doorway.

"But it's not even seven o'clock . . ." Noah muttered. He had trouble sleeping at home; here in this ghostly mansion he was sure to be up all night.

"But what about that cake we saw cooling in the kitchen?" Marvin asked, trying to smile.

"No cake, not for uninvited guests," Mr. Thorne said.

Noah looked toward the door, but Mr. Thorne was blocking the way.

"There are books on the shelf, so you can read before bed. Stay inside." Mr. Thorne slammed the door behind him.

"Hey!" Tori yelled, rushing toward the door.

Noah heard a key turn in the lock. And dread spread in his chest.

"Did that guy just lock us in?" Marvin asked.

Tori jiggled the handle, but it only confirmed what they already knew.

"We're locked in," Noah said. He sat down on the bed.

Tori wasn't having it. She kicked the door. "They can't do that to us. We're not prisoners!"

Marvin frantically roamed around the space, and Noah guessed he was looking for an exit.

Noah was scared, but he knew that if he didn't move, he'd be trapped in this bedroom all night. And he would do anything to get out.

Noah got up and looked out the window. The room overlooked the gravel driveway and the dark forest ahead. It was now completely dark, and pretty scary.

Noah weighed the options. At least they all still had their backpacks. "Does anyone have a flashlight?" he asked.

Both Tori and Marvin shook their heads.

"But we have our phones," Marvin added. "They can be flashlights."

Noah felt flustered when he pulled his old phone from his backpack. "Mine is pretty ancient. I try to keep it off or the battery goes."

"Mine has half a life left," Tori said as she pulled it out her of her pocket. "It's not like I thought I'd be spending the night on a haunted island, running from a creepy caretaker and an evil warden's daughter."

"Ms. Chavez seemed okay," Marvin said as he pulled out his phone. Noah noticed his notebook peeking out of Marvin's backpack and almost reached for it. But Marvin was still clutching his backpack.

"My phone is newer. Maybe we use that as a flashlight, but only if we really have to. Just in case . . ." Marvin suggested.

"We have a long night ahead of us," Noah said.

They all agreed to keep their phone flashlights off as long as possible.

"Let's get out of here before Mr. Thorne comes back," Tori said, eyeing the door.

Noah tried the window. With considerable effort, he was able to crack it, just an inch. Then he pushed with all his might, and it slid up.

"Now what?" Marvin looked down to the gravel driveway below. "We'll break an ankle, at the very least, if we try to jump out."

"I don't care," Tori said. "I'm not staying in here."

Noah pushed his way in between Tori and Marvin and stuck his head out the window. The outside wind was cold and wet.

But Noah saw a way out—in the details, being the smart observer he was. "We don't have to jump. We can climb."

Tori gently pushed him aside and looked out, too. She smiled. "Those vines."

"Worth a shot," Noah said.

Tori was already halfway out the window.

"Slow down," Noah said. He felt a wave of vertigo and nausea wash over him all at once. "I don't like heights." It was on page four. He felt like adding it again, only Marvin had the notebook.

"You can do it," Marvin said. "You made it to the cemetery and up that lighthouse. You're braver than you think, Noah. If Tori and I can make it down, so can you."

That gave Noah some confidence. He was still scared, especially looking at the ground below, which seemed very far down. But Noah wished to join his new friends, more than anything. The last thing he wanted was to be left behind in that cold and dark bedroom.

Noah braced himself and climbed out the window. He grabbed the vines just as Tori jumped to the ground.

Noah felt like he was about to cry, but then he saw Marvin below. Marvin had his back. He stood up for him against Liam and believed Noah could be brave. So Noah hurried, gripping the vines, feeling them stretch under his weight. This was scarier than it looked.

New fear to add to his notebook: *climbing vines.*

Noah laughed to himself, sweating despite the cold.

"Hurry!" Tori called from down below.

"No kidding," Noah muttered. He tried to move fast, but the vines didn't seem to like his tactic. Halfway down, a vine stretched. *Looooong.*

And it snapped, leaving him hanging by his fist from one vine.

That sole vine held on. But then it gave out with a crack.

Dropping Noah onto the hard gravel.

20
Friday, 7:08 p.m.

"OOMPH." THE FALL KNOCKED THE WIND out of Noah. But it also released him of the fear of climbing vines. He did it! Even if he did drop halfway down.

It was okay. He was alive.

"Dude, are you okay?" Marvin asked. He and Tori rushed to help Noah up.

"You shoulda dropped and rolled," Tori said, lifting him by his armpit.

"I'll try to remember that next time I escape from a ghostly mansion on a haunted island," Noah said sarcastically.

That got him a laugh from both Marvin and Tori.

"I think I twisted my ankle." Noah tried to put weight on it, but pain shot all the way up his leg. It was bad.

"Can you walk?" Tori asked.

"I have to." Noah looked up at the mansion. The lights were still on in the dining room, which meant Ms. Chavez and Mr. Thorne hadn't gone to bed yet. They had to hurry, before Mr. Thorne noticed they were gone.

Tori and Marvin started toward the forest path, and Noah followed, but at a slower pace. He was actually looking forward to going into the woods. Maybe there would be a ghost in there. And maybe, just maybe, he would see his mom.

Noah was hopeful. Even with his twisted ankle slowing him down.

Marvin couldn't wait to get away from that creepy mansion—and especially that scary caretaker. He'd rather stay up all night than be locked up. Plus, he had a movie to make! All this ghostly history he heard about at the tour and during dinner at the mansion sparked lots of ideas.

The only question was: What happened during that famous prison escape?

Marvin saw that Tori was almost at the tree line already. He rushed to catch up, but turned to see Noah hobbling.

"You okay, Noah?" Marvin whispered. He slowed so Noah could catch up.

Noah nodded, though he didn't look okay. "Yeah." He looked a little scared, even more so than usual.

"Come on!" Tori called from the trees.

Marvin wanted to tell her to relax, but she wasn't wrong: they had to hurry. Get out of there before Mr. Thorne realized that they had broken out of that creepy bedroom.

He let Noah lean on him for the last part, until they were in the forest and out of sight.

"Now what?" he asked Tori and Noah.

Tori said, "I saw this portrait in the warden's office. Remember that prison guard who helped us get out of the forest, and who we saw talking to the prisoners? That was no prison guard—it was Warden Chavez."

"His ghost, you mean," Noah said.

"Exactly!" Tori said.

"But why did we see him arguing with the three prisoners, back when we were supposed to get on the ferry? They were all ghosts, right? I thought the prisoners escaped, and he tried to get the boat back to shore," Marvin said, looking confused. "In that case, we should have seen just Warden Chavez, not the escaping prisoners."

"Yeah, it makes no sense," Tori said. "Maybe they got it wrong. Maybe he caught them on the shore."

Noah said, "But then why did Warden Chavez drown? And what happened to those escaped prisoners?"

It was a mystery Marvin was determined to solve. For his scary movie, but also because he was stumped by the whole thing.

The forest was so quiet around them, it was almost like it was listening in on their conversation. *Very creepy,* Marvin thought. He would have to add it to his story.

Raven Island will take its bounty. That was what Mr. Thorne said.

"We need a computer," Noah said. "So we can find out more about what happened back then."

As she ducked under a pine tree branch, Tori said, "Maybe if we solve the mystery of the escape, the ghosts of those prisoners will be laid to rest."

"Maybe we can do both: solve the mystery and make a movie." Marvin shrugged. "I also want to know what happened. Don't you?" He felt the cold creep in under his clothes. He wasn't dressed for a night on a cold, ghostly island. "That ghost-hunting crew at the prison, they need a computer to upload the show to the internet, right?"

Noah nodded.

A very soft voice said behind them, "I can guide you there."

All three of them jumped.

Marvin turned and stifled a scream. It was Bea, the bird keeper. In her dark clothing, she looked like she was part of the forest.

Bea said, "Follow me. I know a shortcut."

"Let's go," Marvin said to Bea.

Bea nodded and started into the forest, away from the path. "Stay close," she said over her shoulder. "Or the ghosts of Raven Island will get you."

III
Ghost Stories

21
Friday, 7:11 p.m.

THE FOREST SEEMED TO GET DENSER the longer they walked. Tori felt the notebook cut into her skin. It was her secret, for now. The warden's diary. She wondered what stories were in there.

And she worried what she might read, too. What if there was a bunch of horrible stuff about the treatment of the prisoners? She knew Raven Island Prison was the toughest place to be incarcerated back in the day. What if those kinds of things were happening to her brother, right now?

The thought of it made her sick. The canned soup and stale bread that she ate for dinner were roiling in her stomach behind that notebook.

Bea looked over her shoulder, like she was wondering why they weren't keeping up.

"Noah twisted his ankle," Tori said. "We can't go too fast." Noah was walking on his own, but slowly.

Bea nodded and slowed her pace. Still, she looked like she was one with the forest. As if her feet didn't even touch the ground. And when they got to this crossroads between paths, she seemed to be twirling around the trees. Like she was hiding something.

But Tori was too lost in thought to pay much attention to Bea.

"Are you okay, Tori?" Marvin asked. He studied her face.

Tori was grateful for the forest's darkness, or he might see her expression. Truth was, she wasn't okay. This prison, being trapped here—it all hit just a little too close to home. "I'm fine," she lied.

Bea was far ahead of them now.

Marvin said, "Oh good . . . It just seemed like you weren't when you ran out on dinner. Granted, it was pretty lousy food, so I can't blame you."

Tori laughed. She was grateful for Marvin's sense of humor.

"Just . . ." Marvin hesitated. "You can talk to us, you know," he said. "To me. I'm a decent listener; my sisters even say so."

But Tori felt alone in her sadness. Tori knew she was the only one with a brother in prison. And that made her feel alone. "Thanks," she said instead. "I just . . . I really miss my brother Danny. He used to come to all my games. And he always made me laugh."

"We'll be off this island by morning," Marvin said. "You can see him then."

"Yeah, sure," Tori added with a nod. Only she knew that Danny wasn't going to be home when she got there.

Noah was still trailing behind, but catching up to Tori and Marvin now. "What did I miss?" he asked.

"We were discussing dinner," Marvin said, making a disgusted face.

"It wasn't that bad," Noah said.

"I wish I had your positive attitude," Tori said. She held back a pine branch so the others could walk.

"Turn that frown upside down," Noah said, like he'd rehearsed it. "That's what my mom says."

"She sounds nice," Tori said. At her house, there was mostly a lot of chaos and fighting. With four brothers (now only three in the house), things were always loud—and sports were a big deal in their family. There was football in the backyard on weekends, games on TV all the time, even during dinner. Tori loved it, but sometimes it felt like she got lost in the shuffle between her brothers and parents, who both worked long hours. It was why she missed Danny. He was the oldest, and he always made sure Tori knew that he saw her.

Noah's face was sad. "My mom's dead," he said.

Tori felt like a fool. How come she didn't know that about Noah? It was easy: she barely knew him. He was the new kid who came in midyear. "I'm sorry, Noah," she said. "I can't imagine losing my mom."

"Yeah," Marvin added. "Sorry, that stinks."

Noah nodded. It was obvious he didn't want to talk about it, and Tori couldn't blame him.

They came up to the edge of the forest. Tori looked for Bea, but she'd disappeared.

"Looks like Bea flew away," Noah said, looking up at the trees like he actually believed it.

"She's kind of odd," Noah said, and Tori and Marvin nodded in agreement.

"Let's find the ghost hunting crew's computer," Tori said. She charged ahead, grateful to have a purpose, something to keep her occupied. It felt better to make decisions—it kept her from thinking too much, which was how she liked it.

The journal seemed to burn against her skin. What was inside?

What would the last warden have to say about Raven Island Prison?

22
Friday, 8:11 p.m.

NOAH WAS MAD AT HIMSELF. WHY did he have to go and twist his ankle, when Tori and Marvin were just fine? He was hobbling behind them, hoping that maybe someone from the ghost-hunting crew had an emergency kit so he could tape his ankle. It was not even nine o'clock—there was a whole night ahead of them. And he sure as heck didn't want to spend it locked in the mansion bedroom.

"You okay, Noah?" Marvin asked, slowing down so he could walk next to Noah. Marvin was nice. If there was one good thing that came out of this field trip, it was that Marvin and Tori seemed like they were his new friends.

But would Marvin still be talking to him once this was all over? Noah wasn't sure. Marvin was a cool guy, into movies, wearing the trendiest clothes. Noah's pants weren't even the right size, never mind the right brand. And then there were his huge fears over everything.

Marvin would find out that secret soon enough if he looked at the notebook. Now, *that* was Noah's biggest fear: being found out.

"I'm okay," Noah lied. They were almost at the prison. Noah was looking forward to sitting down for a little while, maybe.

His ankle felt better but wasn't back to normal quite yet.

Tori stood by the open prison door. Bright light came from inside—probably some sort of camera light.

Marvin and Tori waited for Noah to go in first, which made him sweat despite the cold temperature. What if he really did see the ghost of his mom? Noah wanted to, but he wasn't sure if he was ready for it, if he was honest with himself.

But inside, there was Sarah, holding a computer tablet. She rubbed her neck, looking tired. "Hey, it's the stragglers of Raven Island!" She smiled. "We could use you kids to catch some ghosts."

Noah said, "Sure, yeah."

Sarah frowned. "We'll be livestreaming starting in"—she looked at her watch—"half an hour. Make sure you stay out of the camera's shot. Unless you find a ghost somewhere, of course."

Down the giant corridor, there was Tammy. She was working the camera, along with this tall guy who had his back to them.

Noah looked around. "We thought you might have a computer here. With internet."

Sarah nodded. "We have one laptop with satellite internet, to stream the show. But once we start filming, we'll need it to upload."

"Can we borrow it for a few minutes?" Noah asked. He smiled, hoping that would get Sarah to let them use the computer. Otherwise, they'd be out of luck. And Noah wanted to figure out what the history of this prison break was, exactly.

Did they really drown, out there in the Pacific? Or did they get away? And what was the warden's role in it all?

"Fifteen minutes, max." Sarah motioned for them to follow along.

Noah looked inside the cells, hoping to spot a ghost. But all he saw were nasty rooms and darkness.

"Listen, we need to split up," Tori said over her shoulder.

Noah had a hard time concentrating. On the one hand, the cells were giving him the creeps. On the other hand, he had hopes he might see his mom's ghost in there. "Sure, yeah," he mumbled. Then he realized what she was saying. "Wait—why?"

Being alone in a creepy prison was definitely going in his notebook as another thing he was afraid of. In all caps, probably.

"We don't have much time before they start filming," Tori said. "Then we'll have to get out of the way."

That made sense. Noah followed her to the center of the prison, to the guards' station, where a laptop sat open on the counter. It was brightly lit, making him feel less afraid already. Computer research, that's all it was. He didn't need someone to hold his hand for that.

Noah walked over, but Tori was already turning away to split off. "I'm going to check out the other halls. See who all is here, just in case the warden's ghost is present."

Marvin looked longingly at the film crew. "I'm going to ask around," he said as he was already walking away. "See what shakes loose."

Noah was left alone near the guards' station. He took a deep breath. This wasn't scary, he told himself. It was just computer research.

By his feet, he noticed a big box full of old prison costumes. But then underneath he saw something else.

A gun.

Noah took a step back, only to bump into the laptop on the desk behind him. Noah told himself that it was probably just a prop. He stepped closer.

Noah had never seen a gun before. So he didn't know if it was real or some kind of fake. But it gave him the creeps.

Then he heard something. A whistling sound—no, *actual whistling*. It was "Danse Macabre"—Noah knew the sad composition from his piano lessons, back when he still lived in San Diego and took lessons. Didn't Ms. Chavez say that was the tune the Birdman whistled?

Noah glanced around, but didn't see anyone. The whistling faded down one of the prison's hallways. He felt the hair on the back of his neck stand up. Was that Joseph Fink?

Then there was a soft brushing by his feet.

He jumped. But then Noah realized it was just Mr. Hitchcock, the cat.

Noah bent down to pet him. "Dude, you scared the life out of me."

Mr. Hitchcock meowed, then scurried off down the hall.

Noah stood alone by the laptop and looked around the prison. He could see down all five hallways from this guards' station—it was a smart setup. Off in the distance down the second hallway, he saw the guy who was with Tammy earlier unroll a cable. Bob. *The location scout,* Hatch had called him. Tammy was behind the location scout, talking to Sarah.

Noah tapped a key, and the laptop lit up. No password needed—that was not smart, but it made things easy. He pulled up the browser and started with a simple search: *Raven Island Prison.*

That gave him some general information, the kind the school had told them before the field trip.

Then there were a few sites that listed the famous stories: Prison Histories, and the *Ghost Catchers* website (though the history they had listed was on the skinny side).

Noah decided to take a different approach in his internet search: *ghosts of Raven Island Prison.* He hesitated a moment, then hit the Enter button.

Right there at the top of the search results, he saw what he was hoping to find—a dedicated website:

The Ghosts of Raven Island.

And even more specifically:

What happened to the dead? Where are the escaped prisoners?

23
Friday, 8:35 p.m.

TORI FOUND HER WAY DOWN THE hall, back the way they'd entered Raven Island Prison, past the dozens of prison cells. She forced herself to keep her eyes on the exit door.

Out.

She passed Sarah and Tammy, who were deep in conversation about the show's script. There was a guy hunched over, looking at a clipboard. Bob was his name, Tori remembered. He was the location scout they saw during the prison tour.

Not that she cared at that moment. Tori practically slammed herself against the metal exit door, welcoming the cold, wet air outside. Thankfully, it had stopped raining.

She found the picnic bench under the overhang, pulled the journal from her waistband, and sat down.

Tori exhaled. It was almost nine o'clock. She thought of her brother, who was probably in bed right now, staring at the ceiling of his prison cell. She wondered what he was thinking about. She hoped Danny thought of her sometimes.

Danny had been her best friend. He was her big brother, her protector, but also her buddy in a house where there was always chaos and it was hard to be heard. Danny always listened. And he never missed any of her games (even if he sometimes had to leave work early to make it).

But Danny had just made a few new friends. Mom warned him to stay away from them because she had a bad feeling about them, but Danny didn't listen. He was rebellious like that. And now he was arrested as the accomplice in a gas station robbery, but Danny told their mom that he knew nothing about it. That he'd been waiting in the car while the others went inside the gas station that night. He'd sped away once his friends got in, though. So now the police said he was the getaway driver.

The accomplice.

Tori knew it wasn't Danny's fault. He wasn't guilty. But he was stuck in jail all the same. And he hadn't even bothered to call home! Tori felt angry and sad and hopeless. Being stuck on Raven Island didn't exactly help.

Tori shook her head and tried to make those thoughts disappear. She had to forget about Danny. Here, there was this journal—that had to hold some information on life on Raven Island, right? Since it was hidden under the warden's desk, she imagined a warden put it there. To keep it a secret.

Fernando Chavez was the last warden of Raven Island Prison before it closed. And the ghost they saw at the docks. What had happened, that night of the prison break?

Tori opened the journal. The cover felt old, the paper a little brittle and loose from the spine. She'd have to be careful not to pull the pages out.

The first page of the journal had a date and a heading: *First Day on Raven Island.*

My first day was an auspicious one, Warden Chavez wrote

in neat cursive. *The ferry was late because of choppy waters, and we barely made it to the dock before we'd been swept out to sea.*

I thought to myself: God help the fool who thinks he can escape and tries to swim his way out of here.

Then I remembered from the call with the warden who was leaving: there had been two escapees during his tenure, and neither of the men were seen again. It occurred to me that perhaps the locks on the cells, and quite frankly the cells themselves, are unnecessary, if the mere fact of being on the island is a prison sentence.

Of course, then I thought of my wife and daughter, who would be staying with me at the warden's house on Raven Island.

Had I sentenced my wife and my little girl by moving here?

Tori felt a chill go down her spine. She was trapped on Raven Island for just the night, and it felt like a prison sentence.

She thought of Ms. Chavez as a child, in that warden's house with the creepy caretaker who tried to lock them up. Had her stay on Raven Island made her evil?

Tori turned the page. It was dated the next day.

I am praying this evening, and well into the night, for the prisoners of Raven Island, Fernando Chavez wrote.

The previous warden abandoned his post days ago, fleeing the island and leaving me to the task. I toured the prison, shocked to find the conditions unsanitary at best, life-threatening at worst. Dietary norms are a foreign concept to the bug-infested kitchen, full of expired food. Prisoners are told to reside in their cells more than twenty-three hours a day, with little daylight and a mere thirty minutes of exercise a day, also in complete silence. If they do not comply, there is a beating so severe, the prisoner is lucky to be able to stand upright the next day. I witnessed all this and had to run outside to be sick in the bushes.

Only the ravens listened to my cries. I then had to go back inside and see what was used as punishment: a solitary confinement cell underground, used to—

Tori closed the journal and then her eyes. She wasn't going to cry, not over some journal from decades ago. Surely, her brother was living under better conditions. He had to be!

This was ancient history.

And yet . . . what about those faceless prisoner ghosts at the cemetery? What about the prisoners who tried to escape . . . ?

Tori felt like she was staying in the land of the dead. Like it was all bad dream. Tears streamed down her face for reasons she couldn't understand.

Just as Tori was about to get up and join Marvin and Noah inside, she saw a figure. Through one of the cell windows. It was just the very top of his head, but it looked too much like one of the prisoners—that tall man with the bald head.

Could it be the ghost of one of the three escaped prisoners—the tall guy, John Bellini? Those short men they saw at the dock were probably the Smith brothers who escaped, so it made sense . . .

Tori got goose bumps as she watched the bald head disappear. She jumped up and grabbed the journal. Tori was ready to go inside when she got shoved out of the way.

The metal door swung open, and Noah peered out. "Tori?" he called. Right in her face. "Oh, there you are."

She wiped her cheeks from tears, quickly, before anyone could see.

"Tori, are you okay?" Noah asked. He stepped back inside a little, still holding the door, like he knew she needed her space.

Tori was grateful for the darkness. She clutched the journal; she was pretty sure that Noah saw, but he was nice enough not to ask her what it was.

"Do you know where Marvin is?" Noah asked.

Tori shook her head. She wanted to tell him about the ghost she saw, but then started to question herself as they passed the cell.

Noah motioned down the hallway. "Come quickly, before we lose the computer."

She followed him with lead in her shoes because she dreaded going deeper inside the prison.

But then Noah said, "Those prisoners who Mr. Thorne said drowned? I think they're alive. They actually escaped!"

24
Friday, 8:55 p.m.

MARVIN WAS HAVING A GREAT TIME—NOT that he'd ever admit that to Tori and Noah. He was supposed to be questioning the crew about the history of the prison break, but who could be bothered with that when there was such a great opportunity to learn about filmmaking right here?

He'd started with Tammy and Sarah, but those two mostly got irritated. They were planning the ghost-hunting locations with Bob, which wasn't very interesting anyway. Marvin wanted to catch up with Hatch—he was the real star, after all, the real ghost hunter. Sarah told Marvin that Hatch was surveying the prison cells, to locate the energy sources.

Tammy had rolled her eyes at that. But Marvin didn't care. He'd walked past Noah, but he was so wrapped up in the computer research, he didn't even see him.

Marvin glanced down two of the prison hallways before he found Hatch. From afar, he looked so cool in his black clothes, dark hair, and black-framed glasses. But up close, Hatch looked . . . worried.

"Hey, kid," he said to Marvin. "Weren't you supposed to be on the last ferry out of here?"

"We missed it," Marvin said, purposely leaving out the part

where he jumped off that ferry. Marvin added a little shrug, like it was no big deal. "What are you doing?"

Hatch let out a heavy sigh. "I'm looking for dead people, buddy. But I'm afraid they're not showing up today."

"We saw a bunch earlier."

Hatch perked up. "Really? Where?"

Marvin told him about their ghost encounter at the cemetery, and then later at the docks.

Hatch looked like he couldn't quite believe it. Then he said, "That sounds like a residual haunting."

"What's that?" Marvin asked.

Hatch answered, "It's an important moment that gets replayed, almost like a movie on a loop." He paused. "But I thought the warden drowned trying to get the boat *back*, after the prisoners tried to escape. Why was he talking to them at the docks?"

"That's what we were wondering!" Marvin said.

Hatch seemed to ponder that. "Either way, stick around, kid. I could use a ghost encounter, for the show. And ghosts seem to like you."

Marvin glanced around the hallway. There were several cells—in fact, he realized they were standing right in front of cell fourteen. The one where all the prisoners died. "Didn't the Birdman of Raven Island stay here?"

Hatch nodded. He reached out to touch the cell bars, but then seemed to think better of it. He looked inside the cell but still didn't go in.

And Marvin realized something.

Hatch is afraid. Here was the host of one of the first online ghost-hunting shows, and he was afraid of the dead.

Marvin walked inside the cell. It smelled like wet dirt and maybe some animal's pee. "I wonder if they're still here," Marvin said. "Do you think so?"

Now it was Hatch's turn to shrug. He chewed on a hangnail.

Marvin closed his eyes and tried to concentrate on calling the spirits. Even though he didn't really believe in all that stuff. "Prisoners of Raven Island, show yourself," he said, feeling bold.

But there was nothing except a faint creak of the prison cell's door hinges. And far away, Sarah and Tammy's voices.

"I really need some good stuff this time," Hatch said. "The ratings need to deliver. Or else . . ." He let his voice trail. "The show will be canceled, and then we're all out of a job."

This wasn't what Marvin had hoped for. He wanted to learn more about filmmaking, framing shots, and telling a story. But all Hatch cared about was his ratings.

Marvin sighed. And then he heard it:

Whistling. It was very faint, coming from . . . outside.

"You hear that?" he whispered to Hatch.

Hatch froze.

But then it was gone.

"There's nothing here," Hatch said finally as he turned to walk away. "Let's hope we get more once the cameras are rolling."

"Where are you going?" Marvin asked as he left the cell.

"I'm going to catch up with Bob," Hatch called over his shoulder. Marvin knew from his moviemaking that the location scout tried to find the best spots to film. "I'll catch up with you later, buddy. Watch out for those ghosts!" Hatch added a nervous laugh.

"Yeah, sure." Marvin felt lost, standing there in the middle of the hallway. So much for learning more from the film crew. He just needed to catch some ghosts for Hatch.

Marvin looked down the hallway, but Hatch had long disappeared. Maybe if he found this Bob guy, he could learn more about the history, Marvin thought. Maybe Bob knew more about what happened during the prison break.

Marvin went down the hall, hoping to catch up with Hatch again, but he was in deep conversation with Sarah. She shot Marvin an irritated look.

Marvin shot down one of the other hallways and saw this tall guy—that had to be Bob! "Hey, um, Bob," he called, trying not to be too loud, in case Sarah would hear him. Marvin hurried down the hall, but the guy took a hard right at the end. Like maybe he was disappearing into a cell.

Marvin jogged to catch up to him. This guy Bob was the location scout—he had to know all about what happened on the island.

But when Marvin reached the end of the hallway, he realized the guy hadn't disappeared inside a cell. There wasn't a prison cell, but another short hallway. In front of him, Mr. Hitchcock the cat seemed to be waiting. He meowed.

"Hey, kitty," Marvin said softly, bending down to pet the cat. But Mr. Hitchcock just shot away, down the hall. Toward the end of it, where there was a heavy steel door. It was like the cat wanted Marvin to find it.

The door had a lock on it. Marvin pulled at the door handle, but it wouldn't budge. Then he saw another steel door, a little to his right.

Mr. Hitchcock ran away down the hall, back the way they'd come.

Marvin hesitated. But then he turned the handle on the door. And he had to pull, very hard. For a moment, Marvin wasn't sure if he could get this door open.

But then there was a crack. He pulled with all his might, until the opening was large enough for him to walk through. There was a *huff* coming from the space inside.

And it was pitch-dark. But Marvin wasn't afraid of the dark.

At least, that's what he told himself . . .

25
Friday, 9:15 p.m.

MARVIN MADE HIS WAY DOWN THE stairs to the basement. There were lights on, but they flickered every once in a while.

He passed a room that looked like a hospital, with cabinets meant for medicine. He walked by showers (there was a sign, so that was easy enough to spot), and a few other doors that he was too afraid to open. Still, this was a new level of creepy—literally! Marvin couldn't wait to tell Hatch and his crew about it. Maybe it would help them with filming.

There were no windows as far as Marvin could tell. Which made sense, since it was the basement and all.

The lights flickered again, and Marvin froze. Without them, he wouldn't be able to see anything.

The lights flashed on, then off again, and it was so dark. Marvin thought of turning around, but there was a whole other part of the prison down that hall. What if the ghost showed up there?

The lights flickered but stayed on this time.

Marvin picked up the pace so he could check out the rest of the basement. He was dying to get back upstairs, honestly—it smelled dank here and felt sad.

There was an open steel door, thick and with a huge bar that could probably lock the room behind it forever. Marvin hesitantly walked through it. He felt like maybe he was getting in over his head.

But still, he couldn't stop. He was drawn inside.

The room was dark, and Marvin hesitated. Now Marvin wasn't afraid of the dark—he was a horror writer! But there was *dark* as in the kind in your bedroom at night, when you could still make out your dresser and the mess of clothes you left on the floor. And then there was *dark* like the kind in a room with no windows.

He stood outside the room, right next to the open steel door. That couldn't close behind him and lock him in, right?

The light from the hall shone through and inside the room, making it feel . . . okay. Maybe he could take a quick look inside. There was a tiny slit of a window near the ceiling, smaller even than in the cells upstairs.

Marvin walked slowly, quietly, like he was afraid someone would catch him snooping and be mad.

The room felt like a freezer. He shivered. There was no cot like in the other cells—just the cold, hard floor and a rusty toilet in the corner.

Was this a cell? Marvin couldn't believe it. There was virtually no light, just the deepest darkness.

Suddenly, he couldn't breathe. Marvin turned just as he saw the giant metal door swing. Before he could stop it, the door slammed shut.

He was closed in.

The room was pitch-dark. Marvin froze in place.

26
Friday, 9:25 p.m.

NOAH COULD TELL THERE WAS SOMETHING going on with Tori. She was evasive, at times angry but other times sad . . . And Tori was secretive. It was like when his mom got sick and she hadn't told Noah yet, but he knew something was wrong. Noah wished that Tori would tell him and Marvin the truth already.

He was leading her inside, down one of the five endless halls of prison cells. Tori kept her eyes straight ahead, but Noah couldn't help himself. He had to check each individual prison cell in passing to make sure there wasn't a ghost waiting inside.

Maybe it would have been better if he'd kept his eyes on the desk. Because when he and Tori finally made it back there, Sarah had taken his seat and was busy working the keyboard.

"Um, did you keep that tab open?" Noah asked, glancing over Sarah's shoulder. She had an open screen with all sorts of controls and two camera views.

She shook her head. "Can't. It slows the system down." She sighed. "With the forecasted storm, we'll be lucky if the internet holds up long enough for us to broadcast anything at all."

Noah felt his heart sink. It had taken him some deep diving, but then he'd finally found the link to the only website that listed all known prisoners. Including the ones who escaped and were never seen again.

The three escaped prisoners, the ones they saw talking to the warden, were all on it. Noah recognized the one tall guy in a few of the pictures on the website. But now he couldn't show Tori.

"I found them," he said to Tori. "The escaped prisoners."

That got both Sarah and Tori's attention.

Noah went on, "There's this website, Prisoners of Raven Island Families. Basically, it's this group of family members who want to know what happened to the prisoners who died or disappeared while they were detained on Raven Island." He took a breath. Noah wasn't used to talking this much. "John Bellini—that's the big dude's name—he was a prisoner here on Raven Island."

Tori frowned. "I feel like I've heard that name before."

Noah continued, "He was an escaped prisoner, one of the three men who were never found."

"So what does that mean?" Tori asked.

Noah said, "The website had all these stories—sightings of the escaped prisoners, basically. No one ever saw John Bellini, but those other guys, the brothers? They were seen at a wedding once, and at a funeral."

"No way," Tori said softly, like she was keeping a secret.

Sarah looked shocked.

Noah added, "There was this picture of two guys dressed in workmen's clothes, pretending to be gravediggers at a cemetery. But they looked an awful lot like those brothers who escaped, Robert and John Smith."

Tori nodded. "So the prisoners survived after all."

"Looks like it," Noah said.

"Then who did we see at the docks earlier?" Tori asked. "Those were ghosts, right? But if the prisoners survived the escape, how did Warden Chavez drown trying to retrieve the boat?"

Noah shrugged. It made no sense.

Sarah said, "I need to get back to work. But I'll tell the others what you've found." She grabbed her clipboard from the desk and scribbled something on her paper. "Maybe we'll check out that cemetery."

"If it's not too stormy," Tori muttered.

Sarah turned back around and pulled open another tab on the computer. "Where was it that you found this information?" she asked Noah.

Noah rattled off the website. But when Sarah typed it in the search bar, the screen froze.

She groaned. "There goes the internet." Sarah closed the screen. "Sorry, kids. It was worth a try, but I really don't have time for this right now anyway. Maybe you three should just go back to the mansion and get some sleep."

But Noah wasn't going to be discouraged so easily. "This prison was running before computer records were common. There has to be a record of all the prisoners on the island somewhere. Right?"

Sarah shrugged and turned her attention back to the screen. "I have to worry about this internet connection if we're going to have a show at all. But thanks for the tip, kid."

Noah and Tori stepped away from the desk.

Tori jammed her hands into her pockets. "Where do you think the records were kept?" she asked.

"They're probably gone," Noah said. "Since they closed the prison."

Noah looked around. There were hallways with cells that connected to the center of the web (so to speak) where the guards overlooked everything, but . . . it seemed like they were missing entire parts of the prison.

"You know what," he said to Tori, glancing around again, "I don't think I've even seen any showers. Or an infirmary, for sick prisoners."

Tori looked around, too. "You're right. Where is all that stuff?"

Noah looked at the map that they'd been handed. "According to this map, it's not in another building outside." He looked up. The prison didn't have a second level.

"It can only be in the basement," Tori said, staring at the pitted concrete beneath her feet.

"But how do we get there?" Noah asked.

Just as he spoke, there was a loud scream. A person was howling in fear.

Right below their feet.

27
Friday, 9:45 p.m.

MARVIN SCREAMED AS LOUD AS HE could. The first thing he saw when the steel door opened was a camera lens. It was right up in his face, too.

"Aaaarrrgghhh!" Marvin let out a final scream, then took a step back. "Yo, let me out!"

"It's just that other kid," Tammy's voice went behind the camera. "Dang. No ghost."

"Ah, jeez," Hatch called from somewhere out there, too. "This is going to make the fans angry."

Marvin wasn't going to wait inside that horrible place any longer. He pushed past Tammy, past Hatch and Sarah, and rushed toward the first friendly face he saw: Noah. He almost hugged him, Marvin was so relieved. Tori stood back, afraid to even look at the room.

Marvin was shaking. The lights were back on in the hallway, but all he wanted to do was leave this basement.

Tori saw his shaking hands. "Let's get out of here," she said.

They hurried down the hall and up the stairs, leaving the angry crew behind.

"Cut to a commercial break!" he heard Hatch call.

"We don't have enough sponsors for that," Sarah said.

But Marvin didn't care about the crew, not anymore. He was still petrified, and so he rushed down the prison hall, past the cells, and didn't stop until he was outside where he could breathe.

He set his hands on his knees and focused on the fresh air. A raven sat on the picnic bench, like it was waiting for a snack.

"What happened?" Noah asked. He seemed genuinely worried.

"I went down to scope out locations for the crew," Marvin said. He heard the tremor in his voice. "Then I went down the hall and found this room with a steel door in front of it."

Tori and Noah waited. Marvin took another deep breath as he tried to shake his fear.

Marvin said, "Then someone closed the door. And that steel door was heavy! It looked like it hadn't been closed for years."

"You're probably right," Tori said. "It's probably not been closed since they shut down the prison."

"Why?" Marvin asked. He was beginning to feel the chill of the outside air now.

Tori said softly, "That was an isolation cell."

"You mean they put prisoners in there? In the dark?" Noah asked. He looked outraged.

But Tori just nodded. Then she said, "I read up on it. Prisoners called it the Hole. It was an isolation cell, used as punishment. Sometimes prisoners would be put down there for no reason at all. They'd be down there for days, weeks sometimes. With no human contact—just the guards who'd bring them bread and water. With that steel door closed . . ."

"It's like you're dead," Marvin said. "I'd go insane," he added, feeling sick to his stomach thinking of all the people who had been tossed aside down there. Forgotten by everyone.

Noah asked, "You think it was a ghost who closed that door?"

Marvin wasn't sure. All he knew was that he really, *really* wanted to go home. "Maybe it was that tall prisoner. I think I saw him outside."

Suddenly, there was a popping sound, like fireworks but much louder.

And another. The sound was coming from inside.

"What was that?" Marvin asked. He rubbed his ears.

Tori looked toward the prison door. "Those were gunshots."

28
Friday, 10:02 p.m.

TORI RECOGNIZED THE POPPING SOUNDS FROM the few times her aunt had taken her to the shooting range. It was a noise that was fine there—but here on Raven Island she knew it could only mean one thing.

Trouble.

Tori rushed for the door. Then she called over her shoulder. "Come on." She wanted to know what was going on inside. Strangely, she wasn't afraid.

Noah shook his head, but then Marvin pulled him along. Marvin said, "You can stick with me. Let's go see what that was."

Tori held the door. They didn't need to do too much investigating to see where the gunshot sounds came from, because Hatch and his crew were already there. The camera was pointed right at a body, slumped on the dirty prison floor.

Tori charged ahead.

When they got to the prison's domed center, Sarah immediately rushed over and spread her arms. "You kids need to go outside where it's safe. *Now.*"

Tori hesitated, but then all three of them walked back the way they came, with Sarah behind them. Hatch was talking into the camera, and Tammy went from his face to the body and back again. They were filming.

"Who shot him?" Tori asked Sarah.

Sarah ushered them through the door, shaking her head. "I have no idea." The door slammed behind her, and it was suddenly very quiet.

Tori had a sickening realization. "Someone on Raven Island did this."

Sarah was silent for a moment, but then nodded. "We were all doing our own things—Tammy, Hatch, and I. And Bob . . ."

Sarah looked like she was struggling to find the words to finish that sentence.

"Bob. Is that the dead guy?" Noah asked. He looked like he was about to lose his soup-and-bread dinner.

"Yes." Sarah looked pale all of a sudden. "I brought him onto the set. I hired him. Bob has a résumé a mile long, worked on all these award-winning movies. So when he offered to work with us for this episode, I was thrilled." She touched her stomach. "I feel sick."

Tori was getting suspicious of Sarah now. If she brought him onto the set, she had to have some idea why someone might want him dead.

"He was the location scout," Marvin said. "Maybe he found something he wasn't supposed to."

Sarah looked shocked. "I brought him here, I . . . He asked for the job."

Noah asked, "Wait—is Bob short for Robert? And is his last name Smith?"

Sarah nodded.

Tori muttered, "Bob is Robert Smith Junior—the son of one of the escaped brothers."

Sarah looked like she was about to cry. "He wanted to find out more about the island and if his dad could have escaped. Bob had an amazing background in movie location scouting, so I didn't see any harm in his ulterior motive . . ." She looked angry all of a sudden. "I'm going to find out who shot him."

"We can help," Tori said.

Sarah shook her head and yanked open the door to the prison. She pointed her finger at them. "You kids stay away from the set, you hear me? There's a killer on the loose."

And she let the door slam shut behind her.

"It's not a set, it's a crime scene now," Marvin mumbled.

Then all three of them fell silent.

After a good long minute, Tori said, "We just saw a dead guy. A real one."

Marvin and Noah nodded in unison.

Tori added, "And the killer is right here on the island."

29
Friday, 10:31 p.m.

TORI FELT HERSELF GO COLD, EVEN colder than she already was. The killer was here on Raven Island, *right now*.

Noah said, "I know it may sound whiny, but I really want to go home."

Marvin said, "Considering we're on a haunted island with a killer, I don't think that's whiny at all."

Tori frowned. "But we're here anyway. And it's now—what time, Noah?"

"Just after ten thirty," he said, looking at his watch.

Tori nodded like she agreed, even though you couldn't really dispute the time. "Right. So we can go back to that creepy mansion and get locked in, maybe catch a few z's. Or we can figure out who killed that guy." She *was* tired, but her determination to find out the truth won.

Marvin and Noah seemed convinced.

"I'm not going back to that mansion," Noah said with a shiver.

"Me neither," Marvin agreed.

"I haven't been completely honest with you," Tori said. She took the diary out from under her waistband. "I snatched this up at the mansion, in that office you guys found me in."

She put the diary on the picnic table. Marvin and Noah just looked at it for a moment.

Then Marvin picked it up. He carefully opened it. "It's a journal," he said. Noah looked over his shoulder.

"It's the warden's diary," Tori said. She felt extra guilty about not showing them sooner. "I've been reading it. I know I should have told you earlier, but . . ." She stopped because she didn't really know how to finish that sentence.

"My brother is in jail." The words fell out of her mouth before she had a chance to think about it. "The police arrested him for robbery. But he didn't do it! And he has to stay there because my family can't afford bail."

Marvin and Noah both looked up from the journal.

"That's awful," Noah muttered. "I can't believe they can do that."

Tori was crying. "They can do whatever they want, apparently. It can take months—sometimes a whole year before you even get a trial date. And all the while . . ."

"Your brother is locked up," Noah said, finishing her sentence. "That happened to one of my uncles. He was arrested at a traffic stop for speeding, and then there was a mix-up about unpaid parking tickets. But it took forever to get him out. He couldn't even call home while he was in jail, because it costs a bunch of money, and he didn't have it in his account. My aunt was able to get the bail money, but he's still fighting the charges."

Tori felt better somehow, hearing Noah talk about his uncle. Like her family wasn't the only one dealing with this. "Wait—he didn't have the money to call?"

Noah nodded. "That whole prison system tries to make money off the people they lock up. It costs, like, twenty dollars just to make a short call home."

That would explain why Danny hadn't called her. Tori felt her heart sink. She'd been angry with her brother this whole time, and it wasn't his fault.

"That's why you were freaking out in the prison," Marvin said to Tori, nodding. "It all makes sense now."

"That stinks, Tori," Noah said. "Do you know when he can come home again?"

Tori slumped. "I don't know. I haven't visited him." She paused, looking at her beat-up sneakers, and felt that familiar burning sensation in the pit of her stomach. "I'm just so angry!"

Noah nodded. "Because you feel like he left you behind."

Tori looked up at him. "Yeah." It was the first time someone understood her.

"It's not the same, but I'm angry at my friend Kevin," Marvin said. "He moved, and now he's not even responding to my messages."

"What a lousy friend," Tori said.

Marvin just shrugged. "I'm going to make a horror movie anyway. For Indie MovieFest. But I wish Kevin was around. We used to do these things together."

Noah said, "I wish my mom was still here. I'd do anything to be with her again—I'd even go shopping for clothes. At the mall."

All three of them laughed. It was like that burned some of the nervous energy away.

Tori felt better. Some of that weight about her brother being incarcerated was lifted off her shoulders. But then she thought of Bob, dead in that prison. There was a murderer here. It had to be connected to the island.

She said, "The journal is written by Warden Chavez," as Marvin and Noah looked at the pages again.

"The last warden of Raven Island Prison," Noah mumbled.

Marvin looked up from the journal. "Can you give us the short version?"

Tori nodded. "He hated it here, all the cruelty . . . I think he wanted to change things, but he died before he could."

Marvin flipped to the last written page. "'April 18, 1972,'" he read aloud. "That's the day of the big escape."

Tori said, "The day he died off the coast, trying to get the boat back. Right?"

"But how does that help us figure out who killed Bob?" Marvin asked.

"Bob was scouting locations. He also researched Raven Island's history," Tori answered. "Maybe he was killed because he found something. Something that was supposed to stay a secret."

Noah added, "He was part of this group that's trying to find out what happened to the prisoners who died on Raven Island, and those who escaped. His dad was Robert Smith, one of the three prisoners in that big prison break on the night Warden Chavez died."

Marvin handed Tori the journal back. "Maybe someone didn't

want him to keep looking. Like the caretaker, Mr. Thorne."

Noah nodded. "What else did Warden Chavez say in the journal?"

Tori opened it to one of the last pages the warden had written. "Here, it says something about the fourth side of the island, the part we haven't been to yet."

Noah took the journal and read out loud, " 'Raven Island holds many secrets, I've come to learn. Secrets kept by the ravens, and by its caretaker. Today, I found the biggest secret of all. And the key is at the morgue.' "

Tori took the map from her back pocket. "See how there's a fourth part, right here?"

Marvin nodded. "We have the time. It's eleven o'clock."

Tori smiled. "The best time to go to the morgue."

IV

The Ravens and the Morgue

30
Friday, 11:09 p.m.

NOAH WASN'T REALLY HAPPY ABOUT THIS plan. Going to the morgue, so close to midnight? That had to be near the top of his list of things to fear. Never mind the fact that they just discovered a dead guy and they were on a haunted island. With the killer of said dead guy.

They were all beginning to get tired—Noah could see it. Tori had lost her usual fiery spunk, and Marvin was actually rubbing his eyes. This was getting to be a long night. Those beds at the mansion didn't sound so bad, even if it was basically a prison.

But if they wanted to find out Raven Island's secrets and figure out who killed Bob and why, he knew they had to go to the morgue.

Noah was so afraid of the forest. Of how it seemed to be alive, like the island was. What if it grabbed him and swallowed him whole like it had the prisoners? He thought of that story of the missing prisoners, the ones who went into the forest, never to be seen again. And the boots from those missing prisoners that were found in the forest. What if that was true? He was looking for shoes, just in case, but didn't see any. And he still hadn't gotten his notebook back from Marvin.

Noah used to love the outdoors. He and his mom would

turn their camping trips into studies, logging the plants, birds, and trees they saw—even the bugs. Noah had started his ant-colony study as a way to remember his mom.

He kept his eyes peeled now, hoping she would be here. If Raven Island was so haunted, why couldn't his mom be here?

Noah took a deep breath, then decided to go first as they walked into the forest. "Let's get moving," he said, more to himself than to Tori and Marvin.

Marvin tried to stay close behind, and Tori was at the back. Noah hoped the trees would leave them alone this time. Seemed like every time they walked through there, something got them. And Noah was creeped out when he was walking between the trees.

Like the forest was alive.

It was quiet as they continued walking up the path. The pine needles crunched under their feet. Noah picked up the pace a little, despite being tired. The faster they walked, the sooner they'd get to the morgue.

"Are we sure this is the right way?" Marvin asked.

"Yes," Tori said. She had caught up and was now walking ahead of them.

"How do you know?" Noah asked. He walked a little faster so he could be right by Marvin and Tori.

"There's a crossroads, right in the middle of the forest," Tori said. "You really have to pay attention, but it's there."

Noah stopped. "See the trees? If you look closely, there's a line cut into the bark. Right at eye level or so." He ran his hands across the horizontal carving. Noah said softly, "Someone marked the way. Do you think it was one of the prisoners that was trying to escape?"

Marvin shook his head. "Couldn't be. They weren't allowed out, were they?"

Noah said, "It's possible they were. If the prisoners had good behavior, many had labor duties around the island." He'd done a lot of research on the island before the trip, curious about the history of the place.

"Or maybe Mr. Thorne did it, so he wouldn't get lost on his way to torture kids," Marvin said with disdain in his voice.

It was clear that no one liked Mr. Thorne at this point.

Noah said, thinking aloud, "I know where the crossroads is." He turned to Marvin and Tori. "Remember when that bird lady, Bea, was walking us through the forest? I think she was trying to distract us from it. I'm pretty sure there were signs carved into the trees, telling you where to go." His eye for detail was paying off.

"Let's hurry up," Marvin said. "I'm freezing, man."

Despite his fear, Noah took the lead again, trying hard to use his long legs to stay ahead of Tori and Marvin. And to get through the forest faster, since he was still pretty scared. Thankfully, his twisted ankle was a distant memory—he could barely feel it anymore, he was so caught up in their quest to solve the mystery of Bob's murder and the escaped prisoners from decades ago.

The carvings in the trees were faint, but they were definitely there. Someone was guiding the way.

Noah noticed there was a sudden breeze, practically pushing them along. And the treetops overhead? They were curving, closing in on them to block out the faint moonlight that was illuminating the path.

The forest didn't want them here. And the island was trying to trap them, swallow them whole like those prisoners who only left the boots behind . . .

"Too bad," Noah muttered to himself. But if he was honest, he was a more than a little scared.

Noah was terrified. But instead of freezing up, or wishing for his notebook that Marvin still had, Noah looked up. At the swaying pine treetops. *They're just trees,* he told himself. *Keep walking.*

"You guys, these trees are trying to swallow us," Marvin said, cowering a little as he walked.

"It's probably the wind," Tori added as she walked even faster. "Let's just hurry up."

"I'm walking as fast as I can!" Marvin argued.

"There, up ahead!" Noah said, pointing. There was a clearing, just a little bit of one, where the path widened. He stopped and searched the tree trunks.

There it was: a big *X* on one of the trees.

Behind them, carved in the bark of a large pine tree, there was a square with lines through it. "That's toward the prison," he said.

Down another path that was almost impossible to spot, there was the sign of a circle with beams coming from it.

"The lighthouse," Marvin said.

On another trunk, there was the simple carving of a house. "The mansion," Tori mumbled.

And the last tree, right next to the fourth path, had a flame on it. "The morgue," Noah said.

"Why the flame?" Marvin asked. He ran his fingers over the trunk, tracing the shape.

"Because it's where they burn the dead people," Tori said, a little louder than necessary. "The ones who they don't have room to bury."

Marvin pulled his hand away, like the carving of the flame might burn him.

"Come on," Noah said. "Let's go." This path seemed darker than all the others. And those trees were definitely curving around them.

Maybe I'll see my mom, Noah thought to himself. Although at that point, he wasn't so sure he was ready to see any ghosts. But maybe he would just tell his mom about his night here on Raven Island, if he ever made it off. It seemed like the island wanted to eat them alive.

The pine needles crunched under their feet while they walked as fast as they could.

Noah thought he heard a whisper. Right by his ear. He asked, "You guys hear that?"

Marvin shook his head.

Tori shrugged. "It's probably just the wind in the trees. Let's hurry."

But Noah was sure he heard it now. A whispering, voices muttering, right there behind him.

And around him. He glanced left and right, all the while walking as fast as he could.

"Who is that?" he asked. "Who's talking out there?"

The trees whispered back to him.

Nooahhhh.

31
Friday, 11:45 p.m.

MARVIN COULDN'T BELIEVE HIS EARS. HAD those trees just called Noah? It couldn't be. Tori jumped. And Noah, too—he stepped back until he hit a tree.

"Okay, I definitely heard that," Marvin said. There was a tremor in his voice.

All three kids glanced around, but there was nothing to see or hear anymore. Just the wind in the trees, making the trees sway like they were zombies.

And off in the distance, back where they came from, he thought he saw the faint outline of . . . shoes. Placed under a tree, like someone had decided to take them off and climb up the trunk.

Marvin blinked and straightened. He was tired of this place messing with his head. Sure, it was good movie material. But it was almost midnight, and he was cold and tired.

"Let's get to the morgue already," Marvin said. "I want to get out of this creepy forest."

He walked on the dark forest path, with more confidence than he felt in his heart. But sometimes, you just had to pretend in order to make it through.

There was a fluttering to his right, but Marvin didn't stop walking. Not this time.

He looked to where the sound had come from and saw a black shape. At first, he thought that maybe it was a ghost. But then he realized what he'd seen.

Black feathers. A wing.

It was a raven.

The walk wasn't too long, but it felt like forever to Marvin. His legs were sore and his back was aching. He'd been clenching his jaw the whole time, too. By the time they reached the end of the forest, he was ready to drop to the ground and sleep.

But then he saw it.

The morgue.

There was nothing like looking at a building that used to hold dead people to wake you right up. Marvin took in the familiar stone, the narrow windows (did they think the dead would escape?), and the large smokestack toward the east side of the building. He knew what that was for.

Interestingly enough, this building had no vines climbing and devouring its walls. Maybe there was too much death in there.

Marvin pulled out his phone, using the flashlight function to light their way. Which made the morgue look even creepier.

"This place gives me the creeps," Tori said as if she was reading his mind. "But I guess we should go inside."

Noah asked, "Where's the door?"

Marvin decided to go first this time. He wanted to act brave, even if he didn't feel it. If he wanted to make movies, and scary ones at that, he couldn't be scared himself. Right?

Marvin didn't want to be like Hatch: afraid of his own shadow, never mind the ghosts he was supposed to catch.

The cold, wet wind hit him square in the face as he walked around the stone building. It was on a hill, just a little bit, making it easy to look out over the Pacific. The water was a charcoal color, choppy, and very foreboding. Marvin couldn't imagine how desperate you had to be to swim your way out of here.

But then he remembered the solitary confinement cell he accidentally got locked inside of. He didn't even last a minute. Marvin tried to imagine how lonely and scary it had to be in there, locked up for days, forgotten . . .

"Come on," Marvin said, as much to himself as to the others. He found the door. This one was metal, like the others, but had been better cared for. Or maybe just painted more recently.

Marvin pulled the handle, but it wouldn't budge. "It's locked," he said to Tori and Noah. It was as if the wind blew his words right into the ocean.

Tori tried the handle. It wiggled a little, but that was it. Then the three of them pulled all at the same time.

They flew back, stumbling. Marvin caught the door just in time before it slammed shut.

"Boy, sure seems like someone doesn't want us to go inside," Tori said as they rushed through the door of the morgue.

Maybe it was Raven Island that didn't want them there, Marvin thought.

Within the walls of the morgue, away from the crazy wind,

the silence made his ears hurt. It smelled clean, like it had just been mopped with bleach. The room they were in had framed photographs on the wall, like it was a museum.

Tori looked at one of the images. "This is the prison when it opened."

Marvin stepped next to her. There were guys in striped prison uniforms, all with stooped shoulders and resigned expressions. A few feet away, there was a group of guards. One was carrying a baton.

"They're not even hiding what they do," Tori muttered. "They're *proud* of how they beat the prisoners. They think that they're keeping them in line."

Marvin didn't know what to say. He couldn't imagine having a brother in prison. He had two sisters, and even though they weren't perfect, at least they were around.

There were more framed pictures, each another five years ahead, until the last one, which was dated 1972.

"There's Ms. Chavez's dad," Noah said, pointing at the picture.

Warden Chavez was wearing a suit and seemed to glance somewhere off in the distance, just as he had in that portrait at the mansion. Like he was hoping something better was on the horizon, Marvin thought. There was a man standing next to him. Marvin thought he looked like Mr. Thorne, but the picture was so faded it was hard to tell.

And then there were the prisoners. Noah said he recognized all three of the escapees. The tall man, John Bellini, was leaning on a shovel. He didn't look that old, but then this was a hazy image. You could just barely make out their faces.

"This place is depressing," Marvin said, trying to break the mood. "So, this journal says the key to Raven Island's secret is here. Right, Tori?"

Tori nodded. She was still staring at the photograph.

"Let's look around." Marvin headed for a heavy wooden door that was at the far end of the room. He hoped Tori and Noah were following him.

But before he could look around, there was a slight sound of air moving.

Swisshhhh—

And the door was pushed. Right into his forehead.

32
Saturday, 12:05 a.m.

IT WAS A LUCKY THING THAT Tori was a few steps behind Marvin, or he might've pushed her over. Instead, he stumbled back. Tori looked over his shoulder.

"That door," he said, rubbing his forehead. "Someone pushed it right into my face!"

Tori walked by him and had no problem opening the door. "Maybe it was a ghost?" she joked.

"Not funny," Marvin muttered.

"You're right," Tori said. She felt a little bad now. But growing up with four big brothers, you learned to have thick skin and throw the first punch (or joke) every once in a while. "I'm sorry."

But there was no one behind the door, or even nearby. Tori grew silent as she walked into the huge room. It was colder than in the other space.

There was a metal table bolted to the tiled floor. There was a drain by her feet. To her right, there was a wall of drawers. Tori had seen enough mystery shows on TV to know that those held dead bodies. At least, they used to.

To her right, there was a giant door that looked like it was a cooler. Maybe in case there were extra dead bodies?

"This place is giving me the creeps," Noah said.

Marvin was hanging back a little, still rubbing his head from that run-in with the door. "Why are we here again?"

"Because the warden mentioned it in his journal," Tori said. She walked over to the drawers. "He said there was a secret here. 'Raven Island's secret.'" She was beginning to dislike that warden even more, with his words bouncing around her head. Could his ghost really be haunting Raven Island, like everyone thought? They'd seen him on the docks and in the forest, but that was it.

She hesitated, but then pulled the handle of one of the drawers.

"Tori!" Noah called behind her.

"What?" she muttered. "It's not like there's a dead body in here." But she checked anyway. The drawer was empty. There was a strange chemical smell emanating from inside.

She closed it, trying to not look creeped out even though she was.

There was another wooden door at the far end of the room. "Let's go that way," Tori said. "Maybe there's an office there."

Noah and Marvin followed. She could tell they were getting tired, just like she was. Tori wanted to get home, so she could visit her brother. She understood now that he didn't have the money to call. Danny wasn't purposely leaving her behind.

Tori rubbed her eyes to focus. This quest for the secret of Raven Island was wearing her down. What were they going to find anyway? Those escaped prisoners?

Or worse: A killer?

Tori had a feeling that the secret that Warden Chavez mentioned in the journal was a big one. Maybe even one worth killing for. If only they could figure out what it was.

She reached for the knob when she heard familiar voice behind the door.

"How could they just get away like that?" Ms. Chavez said, sounding irritated. "You were supposed to keep the kids in the mansion, so they could fulfill my plan."

What plan is that? Tori wondered.

There was murmuring from Mr. Thorne, something Tori couldn't make out from behind the door.

"You could've given them cake," Ms. Chavez said. "All children love cake, everyone knows that."

Ms. Chavez and Mr. Thorne were getting closer to the door now. Tori motioned to Noah and Marvin to back away.

Tori knew they had to hurry.

Or they would be caught.

33
Saturday, 12:13 a.m.

TORI FROZE. OF COURSE, THEY WEREN'T about to hide in those dead-body drawers. The idea of crawling into a space where dead people once were made her shiver. They couldn't hide in the giant cooler, either. It was too easy to get stuck in there and freeze to death.

Tori, Marvin, and Noah hurried back the way they had come, through the other wooden door. Back to that waiting area with all the pictures on the wall.

Tori took a spot close to the door. The echo from the other room made it easy to eavesdrop.

"You shouldn't have let these visitors come to the island," Mr. Thorne said. "Now we have three kids on the loose!"

"That was just sheer coincidence," Ms. Chavez said. "They stayed here on their own. Those kids are part of my plan now."

Tori was shocked. She knew Ms. Chavez was devious and secretive, but this? Trapping kids? Maybe she was the killer.

"*Your* plan, maybe," Mr. Thorne countered. "Now they're sticking their noses where they don't belong."

"Perhaps," Ms. Chavez said. There was the sound of drawers opening and closing. "If you hadn't locked them up in the bedroom, maybe they wouldn't have felt the need to make a run for it."

It was silent. Tori guessed that Mr. Thorne had nothing to say to that. Served him right for locking them in. So Ms. Chavez wasn't in on that . . . Maybe Mr. Thorne was behind all the bad things on the island.

Tori turned to whisper something to Marvin and Noah just as the metal door flew open. A cold waft of air swirled around the room.

Tammy and Sarah barged in, carrying something big wrapped in a blanket. Behind them, Tori could see a crookedly parked golf cart outside the morgue's front door.

"Coming through, out of the way!" Tammy called.

Sarah gave the three of them a sideways glance. "You kids. Again."

Noah stepped past Tori and opened the door so Tammy and Sarah could get through. It took Tori a second to realize that the giant thing in the blanket was Bob's body.

She stepped back and let them go into the other room, where Mr. Thorne had one of the bottom drawers open.

Marvin whispered, "I guess having a morgue comes in handy sometimes."

Tori couldn't laugh at his joke.

There was another *bang* as Hatch came in through the heavy metal door from outside.

"I think we can all agree, my viewer friends, that this is an *immense* tragedy." Hatch held the camera at arm's length, filming himself.

Tori was careful to step out of his view. She didn't want to be on camera if she could help it. Hatch turned the camera around and started filming the framed photos on the wall.

"Follow along on this journey through the history of Raven Island Prison," Hatch continued in a somber voice. For once, Tori could agree: it was very sad.

Hatch droned on, until he got to the last photograph. "Here you can see the escaped inmates, John Bellini and the brothers Robert and John Smith. I'm sure you heard their cries at the prison."

"Hatch!" Tammy hollered from the other room. "Put the camera down for a second and help us out."

Hatch looked seriously irritated but shut the camera off. "Tammy, I was broadcasting live, you . . ."

He disappeared through the door.

"Now what?" Marvin asked. Like Tori had the answer.

"I have an idea," Noah said. "What if we ask the ghosts what the secret is?"

34
Saturday, 12:34 a.m.

NOAH HAD BEEN QUIET MOST OF the time. Sure, he was at least a little bit curious about the whole secret of Raven Island, too.

But what he really wanted to know was if there were actual ghosts. And right here at the morgue seemed like the perfect place to check.

"You want to go ghost hunting?" Tori asked him, her face in an *Are you kidding me* expression.

"Think about it," Noah said, knowing he had to convince Tori and Marvin. "If anyone knows what's going on, it's the spirits on this island. Other than Ms. Chavez and Mr. Thorne, anyway."

"And that weird bird lady," Marvin added.

"Right." Noah listened for the adults in the other room, but they were still deep in conversation.

Marvin pulled his phone from his pocket. "I still have some juice in my phone. It's kind of basic, but we can do a voice recording."

Noah asked, "What does that do?"

Marvin said, "Sometimes you can hear ghosts talk when you play back the recording. It picks up sounds you won't hear right now. They do it on *Ghost Catchers* all the time."

"Does it work?" Noah asked. He was creeped out, but also curious. What if he could hear his mom?

Marvin nodded. "Sometimes. It's worth a shot, since we don't have any of the other equipment."

"Great. Where should we start?" Tori asked.

The three kids looked toward the room where all the adults were.

"We can try outside," Tori suggested. "Or in here."

Noah wanted to get out of the building more than anything. Plus, a lot of their weird experiences so far had been outside anyway. "Let's get out of here," he said, and walked outside.

At least it wasn't raining. But it was still very cold, so Noah hunched his shoulders. He glanced around. The wind picked up suddenly, like the island didn't want them there.

"We should get closer to the trees," Tori suggested. Marvin was already headed there.

Noah followed, until they were just under the cover of the pines. He still felt the hair on the back of his neck stand up anytime he got near the forest. Tori and Marvin looked uncomfortable, too.

"Let's move this along," Noah muttered, mostly to himself. He hoped a ghost would show up. Maybe his mom was here, looking out for him. Though Noah wasn't feeling her presence, not like he did at home.

He turned on the recorder. "If anyone is out here with us . . ." Noah started to say, feeling a little silly, but that was ghost hunting: you had to believe. And Noah *wanted* to believe, so badly.

Marvin and Tori watched Marvin's phone, like it would show something about ghostly activity. The truth was, you had to listen to the recording later and hope you heard something, a voice, anything ghostly.

The wind blew the dirt on the path, like it was trying to sneak between the trees and grab them. But it was just wind, not a ghost.

Noah continued, "We want to talk to you. Whoever you are. Maybe you're a prisoner, or the warden, or . . ."

"Shhhh," Marvin said, elbowing Noah. "Listen."

All three of them were quiet. There was the wind, for sure. But there was another sound. Creaking, like the trees were talking. Noah was about to tell Marvin that it was just the pines moving when he heard something else.

Branches breaking. The sound of pine needles under someone's shoes.

"There's someone here," Noah whispered. Could it be his mom's ghost?

But then there was a man's voice. "Hello, children."

35
Saturday, 12:51 a.m.

IT WAS THE GHOST IN PRISON stripes, the one they'd seen at the docks. John Bellini. He was bald, with bushy gray eyebrows. And he was tall and looked solid. Not at all how Noah imagined a ghost would look.

"What's your name?" Bellini asked Noah.

"Noah." He forced himself to step forward, to not be afraid. Or at least to fake that he wasn't.

Marvin and Tori said their names, but they both looked a little scared, too.

Bellini nodded. His eyes were really dark, like the choppy waters surrounding the island. "I'm John Bellini. But you know that, huh?"

Noah nodded, afraid to speak.

Bellini seemed to have a dark cloud surrounding him, but it was probably just the forest. There were no ravens.

"You're dead," Marvin said behind Noah.

Bellini laughed, deep and throaty. But he didn't confirm it. He said, "I've been trying to catch you kids alone all evening."

"What do you want?" Tori asked, stepping forward.

Bellini's laugh faded, and his face got serious. "You kids. I want you kids gone."

The forest was dead silent.

Noah said, "The ferry is coming in the morning. We have to wait for that." He shoved his hands in his pockets.

"What are you doing here?" Bellini asked. "Looking for ghosts?"

A dark figure appeared behind Bellini. A short man, round and wearing the same prison stripes as Bellini. He stood right next to his fellow prisoner, and had a tiny bird perched on his hand. It was the ghost of the Birdman of Raven Island.

But Bellini didn't see him.

Noah held his breath. Marvin was close enough to touch his arm. Tori stood like she was protecting a goal in soccer.

Then there was a whistling sound. Soft at first, but then louder and louder.

Bellini heard it, too. He jumped and turned.

The Birdman smiled as he whistled. A raven appeared and sat on the ground right next to him.

Like the bird was protecting the Birdman. And maybe Noah, Tori, and Marvin, too.

Bellini looked . . . scared. But then his eyes got fierce, and he pointed his finger at Noah. "You stay away from the morgue. You hear me?"

Noah felt his legs tremble.

The raven hopped closer to Bellini, and he jumped. Then he repeated, "Stay away!"

And Bellini ran into the woods, until the forest swallowed his ghost whole.

The Birdman saluted Noah, smiled, and faded away. The raven hopped onto a pine branch, like it was making sure no ghosts came back.

"Holy cow," Tori said softly, exhaling. "That guy looked totally like a real person. I wouldn't know those two were ghosts if I didn't know they were dead."

Noah nodded.

His hands were shaking, so he pushed them deeper into his pockets.

Marvin was about to say something when there was another sound.

A whisper.

Goooooo.

They were dead silent.

Then there was the whisper again: *Goooooo . . .*

Marvin said, "Dude, it's another ghost."

Then there was laughter. Tammy's laughter. "You shoulda seen your face, ha ha!"

Noah was not an angry kind of guy, but right at that moment he felt like shoving her.

She'd sneaked up from the other side of the morgue. Now Tammy just stood there, grinning like she was so proud of herself. "*Goooooo,*" she whispered, to make her point.

"Not cool, Tammy," Marvin muttered.

Sarah joined them, then pulled Tammy by the elbow. "Hatch is back at the morgue. Come on." She frowned. "What are you kids doing hanging around here, anyway?"

"They were ghost hunting, *boooo*," Tammy said, waving her hands like she was a ghost.

"We're finding the secret to Raven Island," Marvin said. Noah thought he should keep his mouth shut. One of them could be the killer, after all.

"No, *the key* to the secret," Tori muttered, correcting Marvin.

"What secret?" Sarah raised an eyebrow.

"Maybe they'll find out who killed Bob," Tammy said. She looked more serious now. "I can't wait to get off this miserable island."

Sarah shook her head. "Let the police investigate when they get to the island in the morning."

She sure seemed eager to get them away from solving Bob's murder. Maybe because Sarah killed Bob.

Sarah pulled Tammy by the arm. "Let's get back to work, okay, Tam?"

Noah realized something. "The *key* to the secret," he said, pointing at Tori. They were looking at everything the wrong way.

"That's what Warden Chavez wrote, yeah," Tori said.

Suddenly, all the pieces fell into place. "I can't believe I didn't think of this before," Noah said, smiling. "We can't find the secret."

"Why not?" Marvin asked, looking confused.

Noah said, "Because we need the key."

36
Saturday, 1:09 a.m.

MARVIN FELT LIKE HE DID IN math class, when everyone else got the solution to the problem, but he just didn't see it.

"We need an *actual* key to get to the secret," Noah said when he saw Marvin's confused face.

Now Marvin got it.

"All those extra doors at every place," Tori said. "Maybe the secret is behind them."

Marvin had a eureka moment. "The keys are at the mansion." He pointed to his left, to his right; then he decided that maybe he should just look at the map. "Remember that mudroom with all the keys?"

Now it was Noah and Tori's turn to look confused, but then maybe they just didn't pay attention the same way Marvin did. Marvin was constantly looking for cool shots, things he could use in his movie. The keys at the mansion had caught his eye earlier that night.

Marvin unfolded the map. "We have to go back to the mansion. Before Mr. Thorne and Ms. Chavez do."

"We'd better hurry, then," Tori said.

Marvin looked at the forest path. "But won't Ms. Chavez and Mr. Thorne come this way, too?"

That had Tori and Noah stumped.

"If that caretaker sees us, he'll lock us back up," Noah said. "We can't go this way."

Marvin looked at the forest. "We'll have to stay off the path."

Into the forest, through the trees. As if on cue, there was an owl, hooting. And something scurried between the trunks, in the dark underbrush.

Marvin steeled himself and walked ahead. Into the haunted forest.

When Marvin worked on his movie editing, he used these noise-canceling headphones that made it feel like he was in a vacuum, devoid of all sound. This forest was the same once you were off the path: it was its own bubble on the island.

Marvin rubbed his ears, and so did Noah and Tori. "It's so quiet in here," Marvin whispered.

Noah nodded. "Creepy."

They walked in silence for a while, close to the path but not on it. Marvin tried to keep up the pace; they had to get there before Ms. Chavez and Mr. Thorne. He kept a close eye on the path for that zooming golf cart. He wished they had one, too—it would make traversing the island a lot easier, and faster.

Marvin's feet were sore. He was feeling the lack of sleep and rubbed his eyes.

There was a dark shadow to his right.

"You see that?" he asked Tori. She shook her head and kept walking.

"What?" Noah asked, looking around. But the shadow was gone.

"Never mind," Marvin said. He picked up the pace now, too.

The mansion was still a good twenty-minute hike away—the faster they walked, the sooner they'd be inside.

There was a scurry under the trees to his left. A squirrel, maybe? What could possibly even live on this island, other than the ravens?

Marvin had no idea. And as if it knew, a raven appeared up ahead. It sat on a branch, watching them. Waiting.

"Those ravens are pretty cool," Noah said. "It's like they're following us."

Marvin didn't think it was cool at all. He saw another raven, up higher in the next tree.

He hurried, so the ravens were behind him.

"How much longer do we have to walk, you think?" Tori asked. She slowed and rubbed her leg. "I'm getting tired." And for Tori to be tired, it had to be bad. Noah wasn't complaining, but his ankle still looked swollen.

Marvin almost caught up with her. But then he looked over his shoulder and saw two more ravens. There were four of them now. "You guys, these birds . . ."

Noah looked, too. "They're probably just hanging out. Watching us."

"Bored birds," Tori joked. She started walking again, thankfully faster than before.

Marvin was seriously creeped out by now. Why was he the one who kept having scary stuff happening to him? "In that movie *The Birds*, this is what happened."

"We're not in a movie, Marvin," Tori said. She didn't even

look over her shoulder. If she had, she would have seen that there were eight birds now.

And three more joined, seemingly from out of nowhere. They swooped between the pines, all of them. Some hopped to keep up.

Marvin walked backward. One of the ravens seemed to be looking right into his eyes. Into his soul.

He counted them, those ravens. They got closer—all eleven of them.

And then there were twelve. Marvin heard himself breathe heavily as he rushed backward.

Into a tree. Marvin slumped against the tree trunk as he counted the birds again. There was another one, appearing from the dark shadows between the trees.

Now there were thirteen ravens. And they were coming for him.

V

The Secret of Raven Island

37
Saturday, 1:28 a.m.

TORI HEARD MARVIN YELP. THERE WERE thirteen ravens. They got closer and closer still.

Also, Tori saw something else—or some*one* else, rather. In the woods, farther back, was the ghost of John Bellini, following them yet again. He stared at her, then placed his right index finger over his lips, as if to say: *Shhhhh. Keep the secret.*

Tori blinked. And the ghost in prison stripes walked away, disappearing between the trees.

And suddenly, a dark shape jumped in front of her. Tori watched as Bea moved her arms like a bird. Bea focused her energy on one raven, the one closest to Tori. Whatever it was that she was doing, it worked: the ravens moved back, until they were all in the same area, a few dozen feet away from them.

"How did you do that?" Tori whispered to Bea.

"Poe is the leader. You get her to move, and the rest go, too." Bea gave Tori the slightest of shrugs. "It's what I do. Birds are my passion."

Kind of like soccer was Tori's. She understood that.

Tori looked for the ghost of John Bellini again, but he was gone. Swallowed by the forest.

"We should move along," Tori said to Noah and Marvin with an urgent stare. She didn't want Bea to know that they were headed toward the mansion. For all she knew, Bea could be the killer.

"We're going to the mansion," Marvin said.

Tori almost kicked him in the shins.

But then Bea nodded, like it was perfectly normal. "You're almost there. But why are you off the path?"

"We were enjoying nature. The birds," Tori tried with a smile. She was the world's worst liar.

"Okay," Bea said. "I think they like you, too."

"Felt more like they were attacking us," Noah whispered with an eye on the ravens in the tree. They made some tweeting noises.

"No." Bea shook her head. "They were trying to help you, I'm sure of it."

Tori looked up at the birds. They didn't hurt the three of them, despite what it might have looked like. *Maybe they were protecting us*, Tori thought. From that ghost, John Bellini.

Now the ravens were just sitting there, like they were waiting.

"Good luck at the mansion," Bea said. And just like that, she was gone—vanished into the forest like she was one of the birds.

"I'm so putting her in one of my movies," Marvin said, still trying to spot Bea in the dense forest. "And Poe, too."

Tori realized they were at the edge of the forest. Off

between the farthest trees, she could see a faint light where the mansion was.

"We're here," she said, pointing.

Noah and Marvin fell silent.

"I guess we go inside," Tori said, walking ahead.

Noah whispered behind her, "What if Ms. Chavez or Mr. Thorne is there?"

"They can't be," Marvin said before Tori could. "We would have seen them drive here in their golf cart. They'd have to pass us on the path."

Tori's feet were sore. The thought of yet another walk across the island after they got those keys didn't make her too excited.

But those doors . . . surely, they led somewhere. Maybe they were the key. Or the keys were the key.

The whole thing was really confusing.

It was one thirty in the morning, and Tori's brain was sluggish with fatigue. And they still had to wait many more hours until the ferry could get here. Plus, there was a killer on the island. She had to stay sharp.

The wind was mild at the tree line. The pines and the mansion blocked most of it. Still, it was cold, and Tori rushed toward the back of the mansion, with Noah and Marvin not far behind.

"You think we need to break a window?" Marvin asked.

Tori reached out and found the mansion's back door unlocked. She smiled. This made everything easier. Now all they had to do was take the keys and . . .

"The keys aren't here," she said as she entered the mudroom. The empty key rack seemed to be mocking them.

Marvin groaned. "We came all the way to this creepy mansion! My feet are killing me." He plopped down on one of the benches and groaned again.

Noah sat down next to him. Tori could tell he was thinking.

Tori sat, too. Let's face it: they were all exhausted and looking to solve a mystery that was probably better left to the police when they got here.

"Ah, I see you're back," Ms. Chavez said. She was wearing black silk pajamas and a fluffy robe, and held a steaming mug. "I made tea, if you want some."

"How . . ." Marvin swallowed the rest of his words.

But they were all wondering the same thing . . .

How did Ms. Chavez get here before us? Tori thought back to their walk along the forest path. If that golf cart had passed them, they would have seen it. And Ms. Chavez had clearly been here awhile already. How had she beaten them here?

It was impossible.

Ms. Chavez saw Tori's face and smiled. "You know, you remind me of a younger me. And I can tell what you're thinking."

Tori wasn't so sure about that.

"Come on," Ms. Chavez says. "Let's have some tea. And I'll tell you everything."

38
Saturday, 1:45 a.m.

TORI OPTED FOR HOT COCOA INSTEAD, and so did Marvin and Noah. Each of their mugs were piled high with tiny marshmallows. They were cold and hungry—sugar was the perfect fix.

Tori sat in one of the big chairs closest to the fire. She was chilled to the bone. But she hadn't forgotten Ms. Chavez's promise. "You were going to tell us something?" Tori asked her.

Ms. Chavez nodded gravely. She sipped her tea. "Ah yes, I will." She sighed, then put her cup down. "The truth is that I haven't been honest with you."

No kidding, Tori thought. She drank her cocoa, letting the warm liquid defrost her insides. The room was comfortably warm, but somehow, she had a hard time warming up.

Ms. Chavez continued, "I was just eight years old when my father got the position of warden at Raven Island Prison. He was so excited." She laughed. "And I was terrified."

"I can imagine," Marvin muttered over his mug.

Ms. Chavez nodded. "We had to move here—live on the island—so my father could be available at all times. He was so excited about the opportunity to become warden that I didn't want to tell him how much I missed my home and my friends . . ."

She continued, "I had a tutor whom I visited on the mainland, twice a week. That was it. The rest of the time I was here." She spread her arms.

The smile on Ms. Chavez's face faded. "I remember when we first arrived. I cried and cried. My mother locked me in my room, she got so tired of it. That evening, my father showed me around the island. He liked to take a long walk, rain or shine, every night."

Tori opened her mouth to mention that she'd read all about that in the journal, when she remembered that she wasn't supposed to have it in the first place.

Ms. Chavez seemed to hold her breath, then said, "I was bored as the only child on the island. My mother was busy—the mansion was in disrepair, and she was busy making the household run. So I started to take walks on my own. Around the island."

After a pause, she added, "Something to remember is that many prisoners had freedoms they wouldn't have had if they'd been detained on the mainland."

"Why?" Noah asked.

Ms. Chavez smiled, but it was one of those sad ones. "Where were they going to escape to? The water is too dangerous, and the island is . . . Well, you're familiar with it. Rumor had it some prisoners tried to get away in the early days, but they soon realized their escape efforts were futile."

"Wait," Marvin said. "What about the prison break?"

"I'll get to that," Ms. Chavez said softly. She continued, "So here I was, a little girl, roaming Raven Island. I was careful at first, making sure I stayed far away from the prisoners. But then I discovered the forest." She smiled.

There was a silence that lasted for what seemed like forever.

Then Ms. Chavez continued, "At first, I would just take the path from the house to the prison, to see my father at lunch. But pretty soon, he was also too busy to spend time with me . . ." Her voice trailed. "I was too young to understand that he was trying hard to make changes, to make a difference at Raven Island Prison. To make the lives of the prisoners better. I was a little girl, and I just missed my dad. I was lonely.

"Then I discovered the birds, and the small creatures that lived in the forest. I loved to disappear—at first on the path, but then I wandered away. And I started to notice that time seemed to stop and fly, all at once, when I was in the forest."

Tori sipped her cocoa, which was starting to get cold. The sugar rush made her awake and eager to listen to Ms. Chavez's story. Tori recognized their experience in Ms. Chavez's description of the forest. It was like the trees on Raven Island were alive, and the forest was its own being somehow.

Noah and Marvin looked as tired as Tori felt. But they were both hanging on to Ms. Chavez's every word.

She continued her story, "I began to spend more and more time outside. My mother was happy to see me enjoying nature, and my father was embroiled in the politics of penitentiary reform. He wanted for the prisoners to get humane treatment.

To get rid of solitary confinement, to make it easier for them to communicate with their loved ones back home. To truly give them a chance to gain skills they could use once they left the prison system. And he was trying his best to deal with a crumbling, failing prison. And I was talking to the trees.

"It was a month before my father's death that I went missing. For almost twelve hours, no one knew where I was. There was a search party, with the guards—and even some of the prisoners—out in full force, well into the night."

Ms. Chavez took a deep breath. "It was Robert Smith, one of the prisoners who'd been convicted of fraud, who found my shoes. Apparently, I had gone climbing into one of the trees, and was curled up very high, asleep against its trunk. It was such a traumatic experience that I don't remember any of it."

Tori remembered something. "Wasn't Robert Smith one of the prisoners who escaped?"

Ms. Chavez nodded. "I owe him my life. My father was working toward getting him released, but . . ."

"Then the prison break happened and they all died," Marvin mumbled. "That's so sad, man."

Noah nodded.

"What happened on that night they tried to escape?" Tori asked. "It's called the biggest prison break in the history of Raven Island." She'd read the warden's journal; she knew about the prison and how horrible it was. Tori wanted to know about that last day, the day the journal ended.

Ms. Chavez was silent for a long moment. "I don't know. I

was asleep in my bed. In the room where we set you up earlier."

More like locked us in, Tori thought, but she didn't want to argue with Ms. Chavez. She wanted her to keep talking.

"Do you think it's true that your dad tried to stop the prisoners and got the boat back?" Noah asked.

Ms. Chavez shook her head. "None of it makes sense. I was hoping . . ." She fell silent again.

Tori felt anger boil inside her. "This place was so horrible, those prisoners would rather risk drowning than stay another day." She'd considered giving Ms. Chavez her father's journal, but thought better of it now. This lady didn't care about the prisoners any more than the rest of the world did.

There was a sadness that washed over Ms. Chavez's face, and Tori quickly felt guilty over her anger. It wasn't Ms. Chavez's fault. She was just a kid when all that happened.

"I want to know the truth," Ms. Chavez said, louder now. "I want to know what happened to my father that night."

Marvin said, "That's why you brought the ghost hunters in, isn't it?"

Noah opened his mouth, but then decided to stay quiet, Tori noticed. She would have to ask him what that was all about later.

Ms. Chavez nodded. "I want to talk to my father. Ask him what happened. I know his ghost is trapped here on Raven Island."

"What about the island's secret?" Tori asked. She was feeling fatigue take hold of her, and it was making her cranky. She was tired of the games, the secrets. "What secret are you protecting?"

Just then, a set of lights swooped across the ceiling. The golf cart pulled in front. Ms. Chavez got up and moved the sheer curtain. "Ah, that'll be Mr. Thorne."

Mr. Thorne. All three kids put their mugs down and got up. "We should get some sleep," Marvin said as he backed out of the room. He made an exaggerated stretch-and-yawn move.

Tori almost rolled her eyes.

"Yes," Ms. Chavez said. "You know the way."

They did, but they weren't about to go where she wanted. They hurried down the hall and disappeared into the warden's office, and then they heard something.

There was a rustling sound. And then there was a jingle.

The jingle of keys.

39

Saturday, 2:20 a.m.

NOAH, MARVIN, AND TORI ALL HELD their breath. Noah tried to listen for Mr. Thorne's footsteps, but there was no sound. Mr. Thorne was like a ghost.

What if Mr. Thorne came in here and found them? What if he stuck them back inside that bedroom? As much as Noah was dying for some sleep, that was definitely not what he wanted.

"You think he left?" Noah asked Tori and Marvin. Both looked frazzled and exhausted. Marvin shrugged. Tori shook her head.

Noah decided to take his chances. He opened the office door and peeked out, just as Mr. Thorne walked away.

Noah slowly closed the door. His heart was pounding about a million beats a minute.

They waited for a minute or two, but it seemed like forever. When he opened up the door again, the hall was empty. Noah could hear Mr. Thorne talking to Ms. Chavez.

They had to hurry.

Noah went first, down the hall and to the mudroom. And there it was: a giant key ring with about a dozen keys in various shapes and sizes. The smell of cigarettes still lingered from when Mr. Thorne had been there.

Tori got ahead of Noah and lifted the key ring off the hook. Then she said, "Where are we going?"

Noah whispered, "All these doors seem to be in basements. We have to find a door, at the lower level."

They went back the way they came, past the office, past a door that was a utility closet. Just as Noah thought all was lost, they were back in the kitchen. And he spotted a mysterious door at the far end of it.

They rushed over and opened it—and sure enough it led to stairs going down to a cellar. Noah felt a wave of fear as he looked into the darkness below.

But then Tori turned on the lights, and Noah felt some relief. They walked down the stairs.

The air was even colder as they moved to the lower level of the mansion. Marvin closed the door behind him as quietly as possible. Noah wanted to be at the front, just in case there were ghosts down here. So once they made it down the stairs, he looked past Tori.

No ghosts.

Noah flipped the light switch by the stairs.

There was a very large cellar, with empty shelves lining the walls. Ms. Chavez needed to restock, for sure. A tiny window at the far wall let in no light. And it was definitely not an escape route should Mr. Thorne bust them, so they'd better hurry.

In the far corner of the cellar, there was a dark hallway. Noah walked toward it, feeling all his fears pop up.

Not now, he thought to himself. This was not a time to be afraid.

Noah felt his way down the dark hallway. He let his fingers run along the cold stone. Just yesterday, he would've been worried about bugs, rodents, and whatever else creepy his mind could conjure up. But now he was too focused on looking for a door.

Finally, his hand felt the end of the wall. Hinges. And a heavy metal door, just like at the morgue, the lighthouse, and the prison.

"This is it," he said.

Tori pulled out the key ring. "Finding the right key might take a while," she said. She started with the shinier ones.

"Try the older ones," Noah suggested. "This door has to be old, too."

"Good idea," Tori said with a nod. She let her fingers run down the ring, until she reached one of the rusty keys. No dice.

Suddenly, Noah thought he heard a door open behind him. The cellar door.

Marvin heard it, too. He froze, and even in the dark Noah could see that he was terrified.

"Are you brats down here?" Mr. Thorne's voice called.

Tori fumbled and dropped the keys. Quickly, she picked them up.

Noah pointed to the largest, oldest-looking key. They were out of time!

Tori put the key in the lock and . . . it turned! The door opened slowly—it took all three of them to pull it open.

But they had good motivation: Noah could hear Mr. Thorne's clunky footsteps on the stairs.

Behind the door, there was more darkness. But there was also another hallway—or more like . . .

A tunnel!

Two old bicycles were parked on the side.

"I know you're down here!" Mr. Thorne called. He was no longer on the stairs. They had to hurry.

Noah hadn't ridden a bike in years, but he figured it was like . . . riding a bike. You never forgot—that's what people said, right?

So he took one bike, and Tori snatched the other. Marvin hopped on the back of Tori's.

And they rode down the tunnel and into the darkness.

40
Saturday, 2:31 a.m.

MARVIN USED THE LIGHT ON HIS phone to guide the way. Thankfully, he'd remembered to turn on the video this time, so he was filming (however wobbly it was) the whole bike ride in the tunnel.

Tori and Noah had to stoop as they biked because the tunnel was so low. There was a metal bar that ran along the right side of the wall with lights, but there was no way to turn those lights on as far as Marvin could tell. Especially not now, when they were zooming through the tunnel.

Just as Marvin's butt was beginning to hurt from sitting on the bars of the rear seat, they reached an intersection. Four tunnels met in the center—one tunnel for each section of the island. There were signs drawn on the walls to tell where each of the tunnels went, just like the ones aboveground, etched in the bark of the trees.

"Now what?" Marvin asked. He turned off the video but kept his phone's light on. It really was pitch-dark down here.

Tori said, "In the journal, Warden Chavez mentioned that he would climb the lighthouse. Maybe that will give us some answers when it comes to what happened the night he died."

"How about Bob?" Noah argued. "Aren't we solving his murder, too?"

"They're connected, right?" Marvin said. He wasn't sure if that was true, but it was a good guess. "I think we can assume that Bob saw something as he was scouting locations. He was killed for it. The mystery of his murder is connected to the prison break all those years ago."

Noah nodded. Tori got back on her bike and pointed straight ahead.

"To the lighthouse!" Marvin said jokingly, punching his fist in the air. But no one felt very humorous. So he just got on the back of Tori's bike again and filmed.

There was another door, not surprisingly. The same key fit its lock—the one big old rusty key was a master key for all the doors.

"Who do you think dug all these tunnels?" Marvin asked as they climbed the stairs.

"This used to be a fort, way back in the day," Noah said. "The military probably dug these in secret, long ago."

"How do you know that?" Marvin said as the cold lighthouse air hit his face.

"Research." Noah shrugged, like everyone did their homework.

Marvin realized that maybe he needed to do some more digging into the island's past—he could use it in his movie. "Hey, can we lock the door behind us? Mr. Creepy is probably running to catch up with us right now."

"Good point." Tori went back down the stairs and locked the door.

Marvin looked at the spiral stairs that went up to the

lighthouse tower. It made him dizzy, so he looked at Tori and Noah instead. Both seemed tired but charged from the bike ride. "So what does the journal say about Warden Chavez's walk?"

Tori nodded and pulled the journal from her waistband. "He talks about it somewhere toward the beginning . . . Here." She pointed to a passage.

February 21, 1972
I'm discovering more about the island during my walks. Each day I traverse a different quadrant.

"That means one of the four sections," Noah said. Marvin wanted to tell him that he knew that, but the truth was he didn't. They continued reading over Tori's shoulder.

The lighthouse truly has the best vantage point. I have already discovered that the boat dock is not well patrolled. I must discuss this with my guards. I can see the prison from the top of the lighthouse. How dreadful the place looks, even from far away. I am torn between my duty as a warden and my conscience as a fellow human. I must find a way to change our prison system, and the start is right here on Raven Island. I shall make a difference for those men.

The three kids were silent. Tori turned the page. "That's it. He drowns the next day, trying to retrieve the boat after the prisoners' escape. Supposedly."

Marvin felt a deep sadness spreading from his chest. He could only imagine how Tori felt.

"You know that people who look like me are six times more likely to end up in prison than a white person?" Noah said. He looked angry and sad all at once.

"Really?" Marvin said. "That's wrong, man." But he also knew there was plenty of hate and injustice against Asian people like him. He'd been called names in school, and his grandma once got harassed at the grocery store when Marvin was little.

Noah said, "My mom and I went to a Black Lives Matter protest, and I learned all these facts, these statistics . . . Man, it's bad for Black people all around. Never mind if you end up arrested." Noah added softly, "My dad won't even let me walk home alone if it's dark out. You're right: that's really wrong." He paused. "I miss my mom. She always knew how to talk about this stuff and put it in perspective."

Marvin said, "It's bad for Korean people, too. My grandma always tells me, 'Behave, Marvin.' Like I have to be extra good, or I'll end up in . . ." He shrugged. "You know, a place like your brother Danny, Tori."

"It's all wrong." Tori closed the journal. "Even Warden Chavez knew it. But he *wanted* to do something. That's pretty obvious from his journal. Only he died before he could."

Marvin looked at the dizzying staircase. "So he would have walked here the night he died, right? Or ridden a bike."

"I think he walked aboveground when he went on his evening strolls, not that it matters so much," Tori said. "In the journal, he talks about the ravens."

"But he would've gone up here in the lighthouse, right?" Marvin asked. He started up the stairs. "Maybe if we go up to the tower, we'll be able to retrace his steps and figure out what happened."

Marvin climbed the spiral staircase, his sneakers squeaking against the metal. He was going fast, determined to get up to the top and see what Warden Chavez had seen.

Tori and Noah (with their long legs) were right behind him. When they finally reached the top, Marvin's calves felt like they were on fire.

Warden Chavez was not wrong: you could see the whole island from up here. Marvin saw the morgue, the mansion, and the square of forest that marked the island with a giant X, dividing each section.

And there was the prison. It did look like a miserable place, like a dead squid splashed out with its tentacles in all directions. The bell tower was covered in bird poo, and Marvin was pretty sure he spotted a raven perched on top. Those birds still gave him the creeps, no matter what Bea might've said about the ravens protecting the three of them.

Down below was the cemetery. It was lit by moonlight, and without the faceless ghost prisoners it didn't look so scary.

"The boat dock," Noah said, pointing toward the west side of the island, near the prison. "You can see it plain as day, even in the dark."

"What if he saw the prisoners that night?" Tori said slowly.

"Maybe he went to bust them . . . ?" Noah seemed unsure. "It's what they said happened, right?"

"It's out of character," Marvin said. This was the one thing he was an expert on: with his moviemaking and storytelling, he'd learned all about character motivation. Of course, Warden Chavez wasn't a character in one of his movies, but still.

Tori and Noah looked at him.

Marvin pointed to the journal that Tori was clutching. "His last words were literally: I'm going to change things."

" 'I shall make a difference for those men,' " Tori said, correcting him.

"Exactly! Does that sound like a guy who's going to bust these escaping prisoners?" Marvin asked them. "No, of course not."

"But what did he do, then?" Noah asked, scratching his head. "We saw those ghosts at the dock, the warden talking to them. Especially that ghost of John Bellini we keep seeing around the island. I wonder what actually happened . . ."

Marvin said, "Warden Chavez saw those three guys trying to escape from up here. Then he went to stop them and then . . ." He sighed. "I don't know. Maybe he hid them. But they disappeared, right?"

Noah nodded. "Where would you hide three prisoners, though?"

All three of them were silent as they thought about it. Marvin tried to imagine what he would do if he were the warden and was trying to hide three grown men in prison stripes. The forest seemed like the place, but that would be cold and dangerous. If Marvin were in the warden's shoes, he would try to hide them somewhere no one would look.

Maybe . . . maybe Warden Chavez had the same crazy idea Marvin did.

Marvin smiled because he thought of the best, most ridiculous place. "If I were a warden, I know where I would hide three escaped convicts. Where no one would look."

Tori and Noah looked at him.

Marvin smiled and said, "At the morgue."

41
Saturday, 3:20 a.m.

THE STORM WAS GATHERING STEAM. NOAH watched the wind whip around the lighthouse, like it wanted to devour the tower with the three of them in it. This was some weather, nothing like he was used to growing up in San Diego. And none of them were dressed for it.

But for once, Noah didn't feel terrified. Sure, he was a little anxious about getting rained on and being cold, but it wasn't that full-blown terror that gave him panic attacks. He hadn't thought of his notebook in a while now. That had to be a good sign.

Noah looked out the lighthouse's windows.

"Should we try to take the tunnel to the morgue?" he asked Tori and Marvin. It was raining, too—hard rain that came down in sheets.

Marvin shook his head. "Caretaker Dude is probably waiting for us down in the tunnel. We don't have a choice: we have to take the aboveground route."

"We can walk through the forest," Tori said with hesitation. It was a bad option. They all knew it. Those trees might swallow them whole.

Noah went first down the spiral stairs. He smiled to himself.

Boy, did he have stories to tell his mom now. But was she really there listening? Or did he just imagine her presence? Noah wasn't sure. He wanted to see her ghost so badly.

Lost in thought, Noah had reached the ground without having a panic attack. He smiled to himself just as the door flew open.

A bright light shone right in his face.

"And viewers, hold on to your fears while we enter what could well be the most haunted part of the island," Hatch said, talking to the camera. He turned around and jumped. *"Aaarghhh!"* Then he frowned. "Oh, it's one of you kids." Hatch said the last words like Noah was something you found stuck to your shoe.

Tammy lowered the camera with a sigh. "I cut just before, Hatch."

Hatch shoved Noah out of the way. "Professionals coming through, kid. Get out of the way."

"Dude, watch your attitude," Marvin said, stepping in front of Noah. "Don't mess with my friend."

"Yeah," Tori added as she reached the now-crowded entry to the lighthouse. "We have a right to be here, too."

As Hatch examined the spiral staircase, Tammy gave the three of them a kind smile. "He's just a pain in the you-know-what when he's filming. With this murder, the view count is through the roof, even though it's the middle of the night."

"So that murder worked out for you, huh?" Tori asked, her chin jutted.

Tammy shrugged. "If *Ghost Catchers* is canceled, we're all

out of a job: Sarah, Hatch, and me." She seemed to realize what she was saying. "But we're not killers—jeez!" She laughed, but there was a nervous edge to it.

"Tammy!" Hatch hollered, like he was calling his dog.

"Yeah," she muttered with a sideways glance at the kids. "You guys should probably stay out of the way."

Out of Hatch's way was what she really meant, but Noah wasn't about to say anything.

"Hold up," Tammy called as Noah held the door. "Do you kids know what's up with all these metal doors? There was one at the prison, then there were two at the morgue, and now there's another one at the bottom of the stairs."

Noah just shrugged. "No idea. We're just trying not to get in the way."

Tori gave Tammy a grin as they left the lighthouse.

Outside, the three of them didn't feel so smart anymore. The wind was strong enough to blow you away—in fact, Marvin looked like he was practically being lifted into the air. Rain hit Noah in the face and muddled his view. He wiped his face with his sleeve and pointed toward the trees. "Let's go!"

Through the rain and gale-force wind, they ran past the cemetery, into the trees. There was a lone raven overhead, perched on one of the lower branches, like it was watching out for them.

Noah was feeling a little less afraid since Bea had told them more about ravens.

"Let's walk alongside the path," Tori suggested. "Just in

case any random adults decide to get in our way."

Noah wasn't sure if she was joking about the adults. But as they walked, he did think about the fact that there was a killer on the loose. "Who do you think killed Bob?" he asked.

"Ms. Chavez," Tori said without hesitation.

"Mr. Thorne, without a doubt," Marvin blurted out at the same time.

"Okay, why?" Noah asked. "You first, Tori."

Tori held a pine branch back so they could pass. The forest was denser here, but it sheltered them from the rain and wind. "She was hiding the secret of these tunnels, but I'm not sure why that would be a big deal. Or maybe her father's role in the prisoners' escape?" Tori shrugged. "I just think she seems guilty."

"That's not actual guilt, though, is it?" Noah asked.

Tori's face got red as a tomato. "Oh my gosh, I just did what people did to my brother: I assumed Ms. Chavez was guilty because she acted like she was hiding something."

They were all silent for a few minutes. Noah said, "I've done that, too, Tori. But maybe we should look at the facts instead." Noah added, "It's like a scientific inquiry."

Marvin said, as he ducked under another branch, "The truth is that we don't have all the facts. It could've been anyone."

Noah nodded. He sidestepped a puddle. "So Bob uncovered a secret. Maybe it was the tunnels?"

Tori shook her head. "He would've had to have the keys. Right?"

Marvin nodded. "Maybe there's another set."

"What about the Bird Lady?" Marvin asked. "If we're looking at everyone."

"True." Noah mused, "Without knowing what Bob knew, there's no way to figure out who did it."

The raven followed them. Noah felt strangely comforted by the bird.

He thought of the ghost hunters. "What about the *Ghost Catchers* crew? Could one of them have motive to kill Bob?"

Marvin shrugged, and Tori said, "Sure. I guess."

Noah added, "The ratings are good news for them, that's for sure."

Just as they reached the edge of the forest, Noah remembered something. "Did you hear what Tammy said about the morgue?"

"About us getting out of their way?" Marvin asked with a frown. "Those movie people take themselves *waaaay* too seriously."

"No, about the metal doors," Noah said. "Tammy mentioned there were *two* at the morgue."

"We know what the one door goes to," Marvin said. "That tunnel system."

Noah nodded as they looked at the morgue, which was getting pummeled by rain. "I wonder what the other door leads to."

42
Saturday, 4:01 a.m.

TORI PAUSED AS THEY STOOD OUTSIDE the morgue. She felt a sense of dread. Whatever was waiting for them inside, it wasn't good.

"You guys," Tori said, squeezing that stress ball she had in her pocket. She hated to admit it, but that thing actually helped. "I don't know about this."

"What about the second door?" Marvin asked her. His beanie was soaked, and his eyes were red from lack of sleep. "What if that's the answer to the mystery?"

He had a point. Tori knew that they were close to solving the mystery of the biggest prison break in history. What if those three men had hidden right here at the morgue? It was a smart plan.

And yet . . .

Tori felt like she had cement in her (very wet) shoes. But she straightened her spine anyway, because that's what she did. "Let's go."

All three of them marched toward the morgue, like they were on a mission. And they moved fast—the rain was still coming down in buckets, and the wind made the water feel like ice.

Tori pulled the door. The keys jingled in her pocket.

Inside, it felt warmer. Maybe someone had finally turned on

the heat. Or maybe it was just *that* cold outside. They shook the water off their clothes in the entry. Tori felt silly now for having that sense of dread. It was fine in here, nothing bad going on at all. It was just a morgue.

"So where was the second door?" Tori asked Marvin.

He shrugged. "I heard Tammy mention it. I don't remember seeing any doors."

Tori didn't remember seeing one of those locked steel doors in the morgue, other than the one that was clearly a cooler of some sort. But there was that other room where they'd heard Mr. Thorne and Ms. Chavez talk . . .

"I think I know," she said to Marvin and Noah, and opened the door to the morgue. Like it was no big deal. Like the dead man, Bob, wasn't in one of those drawers, waiting for the police to come in the morning.

The morgue felt . . . different. Like there was someone there—an *alive* person. But the space was empty, so Tori shook off her sixth sense with a little irritation. There was no one here. Her mind was playing tricks on her.

She opened the door to the other space, and just as all three of them entered, she smelled that familiar scent of cigarettes.

"Gotcha," a gravelly voice went behind her. It was Mr. Thorne.

Tori tried to reach behind her, but Mr. Thorne moved away. "I have a Taser pointing right at your back, *missy*."

Noah and Marvin looked worried and confused. Then both their expressions went to angry.

But Tori wasn't angry or scared.

She was fast. People looked at her and assumed that all she did was block the ball as a goalie. But in order to do that you had to be quick on your feet.

She moved her weight to the front of her feet.

Tori swooped around. And reached to snatch the Taser from Mr. Thorne's hands.

Tori said, "No one calls me *missy*, Mr. Thorne."

43
Saturday, 4:16 a.m.

ONLY TORI DIDN'T GRAB A TASER from Mr. Thorne's hands. Mr. Thorne was fast, too, and stepped away from her. That's when Tori saw that he was holding a flashlight.

Mr. Thorne was flustered, despite his waxy-looking skin, and stepped back again. Right into the wall of drawers—one with the dead body in it. He realized it and jumped with a squeal. *"Gaaaahhh!"*

"Wait—you were trying to hold me hostage with a flashlight?" Tori asked. She laughed. "Now, *that's* pretty funny."

"I'm glad you think so," Noah muttered. He still looked scared.

But Tori saw Mr. Thorne for who he really was: an old, scared man who thought he was protecting a secret. He had to have known about the tunnels all along. Maybe Ms. Chavez made him keep the tunnels hidden.

"We know your secret," Tori said. Her voice echoed off the morgue's walls.

Mr. Thorne froze. He still held out his flashlight, like it could protect him somehow.

"We know about the Raven Island tunnels," Tori went on. "How they connect all four corners."

Mr. Thorne exhaled, like he was relieved. "Right. The tunnels on the island." He looked at his hand and realized he was still pointing the flashlight. He tucked it into his coat pocket. "They were here when I joined the staff. A holdover from when Raven Island was a fort during the Civil War. There was some cleanup and repair, but overall, it was a nice perk. No need to deal with the rain, or those ravens." He said the last words—*those ravens*—like he was speaking about a pest.

"I like the ravens," Tori said. She realized she had her hands on her hips but didn't care. "They have been nicer to us than most of the humans on this island. Sure, maybe they're birds, and they seem a little scary at first. But they take care of the island. Which really is your job, Mr. Thorne."

Her words echoed off the metal drawers; then it was silent.

Mr. Thorne cleared his throat. "You're right. I'm terrible at my job."

"I don't think Tori meant that, exactly," Marvin said softly. "Just don't lock kids up and hold them hostage and stuff."

"Yeah," Noah added.

"And tell us where that second door goes," Tori added, feeling emboldened by her own speech. "The truth this time."

Mr. Thorne looked terrified all of a sudden.

"Is that where the warden hid the prisoners?" Tori asked. She was pretty sure she'd figured out that that was what happened. "We went to the lighthouse and saw what he would have seen on one of his evening strolls. The prisoners were going to steal the boat and row to the mainland," Tori continued. She could picture it now: Warden Chavez, who hated his own prison system, watching three prisoners want to get out so desperately that they'd get into a rickety boat rather than serve out their time.

"It was certain death," Mr. Thorne said softly. "Anyone knew that. But he should've simply detained them! Sent them back to their cells!"

"Did you see those cells?" Tori asked, feeling a mixture of anger and sadness boil inside her like a thick stew. "No daylight but for a tiny slit of a window. No talking, no space, with only a half hour of outside time, often locked in with another prisoner who's as angry and scared as you."

Tori continued, "And those escaped prisoners? They were probably looking at solitary confinement, right?"

No one spoke.

"Right?" Tori asked Mr. Thorne again. She knew it was true. "Plus, Warden Chavez felt like he owed Robert Smith for finding his daughter when she went missing in the forest. So the warden did the only thing he could do: he hid them. Then he somehow smuggled the prisoners off the island, I don't know . . ." Her voice trailed.

"That's impossible," Marvin said. He pointed in the general direction of the docks. "They had guards to keep that from happening. Even if he was the boss, Warden Chavez couldn't possibly get them on the ferry. Three grown dudes!"

Noah nodded. "So how did he do it? Or did they die or something?"

"I know!" Tori said, pointing to the drawers. "He smuggled them off as dead bodies!"

"There are ovens for the dead," Noah said softly. "If you died on Raven Island, you were either buried or cremated. Even the dead didn't get to leave."

That made Tori's stomach turn, yet again.

Mr. Thorne shook his head and started walking toward the back door in the morgue. "Come on, I'll show you what Warden Chavez did."

They followed Mr. Thorne, Tori taking the lead. Mr. Thorne's shoulders were stooped, like he was carrying an invisible weight on his back.

Mr. Thorne stopped in front of the two doors. "As you know, the door to your left leads to the other corners of Raven Island. This other door . . ."

"Does it go to the docks?" Noah asked.

Mr. Thorne unlocked the door with his own old key, but this one looked slightly different. Shinier, for one, like someone had taken care of it. He shook his head as he pulled the heavy metal door open. "Just watch."

The door opened to a small hallway, and at the end of it there was another door. He unlocked that one, too, with a different key. "You need both keys," Mr. Thorne said. "Only myself and the warden have both."

"This is the real secret of Raven Island," Tori whispered.

Mr. Thorne nodded.

Marvin was still looking confused, but Noah just figured out what Tori had.

"No way," Noah muttered.

Tori said, "This tunnel goes to the mainland. Warden Chavez didn't go looking for the prisoners when he tried to bring that boat back. He helped them escape. He just let them walk out."

44
Saturday, 4:35 a.m.

MARVIN FELT LIKE A FOOL. HE was the last one to get it: here there was this tunnel to the mainland, one that helped the three prisoners escape. *This* was the big secret.

Marvin frowned as they looked into the dark tunnel. "Wait—we could have gone home through this tunnel yesterday?"

Mr. Thorne shook his head. "The tunnel caved in some years ago. Ms. Chavez doesn't know about the tunnel to the mainland. The key to the door was always there, but she never used it." He let his words hang in the air.

"So Ms. Chavez doesn't know that the prisoners got out this way?" Marvin asked. He was pretty sure she didn't. Ms. Chavez still thought that her father drowned out there in the Pacific, trying to get a boat.

Marvin could see the whole thing play out like a movie: Warden Chavez saw the prisoners, decided to save them, and took them to the tunnel. As he imagined the scene, Marvin said, "Warden Chavez helped them escape, then went back to the docks to cover it up. He made it look like they drowned in the currents."

Mr. Thorne was actually crying. "I had no idea. I guessed, but . . ."

"You didn't want to make Warden Chavez look bad," Marvin added. He could imagine that, too.

"I had to keep the secret," Mr. Thorne said. "That morning after the prison break, I found the door unlocked, and I knew the prisoners somehow got the warden's key. I guessed Warden Chavez gave it to them." He added, "Thankfully, Ms. Chavez never knew that it was her father who helped them escape. She didn't know that the tunnel was here. I kept Raven Island's biggest secret."

"Why?" Marvin asked.

"To save Warden Chavez!" Mr. Thorne said, his voice cracking. "If it was uncovered that he helped those prisoners escape, his reputation would be destroyed. There would be no money for young Ms. Chavez and her mother. Warden Chavez would've been disgraced."

"Instead, he was the hero," Tori mumbled. "He tried to stage the boat to make it look like the prisoners drowned, but instead . . ."

"He drowned by accident," Marvin said, finishing her sentence. "Dude, I couldn't make that up, not even for a movie."

"And now the secret is out," Tori said, exhaling the words like she had been holding the secret inside herself. But Marvin knew why she cared so much.

"So what about the murder?" Marvin asked, thinking that maybe they could solve another mystery while they were on a roll.

Everyone looked confused.

"Bob's murder." Marvin shrugged. "It makes sense that he was killed to keep the secret, right?"

Everyone looked at Mr. Thorne.

"I have nothing to do with that man's death," Mr. Thorne said, sounding like his old grumpy self again. He wiped his cheeks. "Nothing."

"But couldn't Bob have found the doors when he was scouting locations?" Marvin asked Mr. Thorne, watching the man lock up the secret tunnel to the mainland. "Wasn't that also a secret you were trying to protect? Ten minutes ago, you were ready to tase Tori in the back."

Noah added unhelpfully, "Technically, it was just a flashlight."

Tori still looked a little bowled over by the uncovering of Raven Island's secret. She kept staring at the door.

Mr. Thorne unlocked the other door, the one that connected the four corners of the island. "I'm going to make sure that ferry gets here on time. I want you kids out of here by daybreak."

And Mr. Thorne closed the door.

"Technically, it's not daybreak, but midmorning," Noah said to the closed door.

It was just the three of them again. The silence of the morgue was scary somehow, Marvin thought.

"Now what?" Marvin asked no one in particular, just to break that silence.

"There's still a dead guy in the drawer," Noah said.

Tori added, "And a murderer on the loose. Any one of the people on this island could've killed Bob. There's no way we can figure out everyone's motives and all that detective stuff."

"We can try," Noah muttered.

"There's not enough time, dude," Marvin said. He felt disappointed, like they had failed somehow.

Tori laughed. "A tunnel to the mainland—who could make that stuff up? It's like some sort of movie."

"Yeah." Marvin laughed a little, too. Tori was right. But he also felt an idea forming, one that could be stupidly ridiculous. Or brilliant.

"What?" Noah asked him.

Marvin knew his excitement was written all over his face. "I have an idea," he said, a little louder than expected. His words filled the morgue. "I know how we can catch the killer."

Tori and Noah both looked at him. Behind them, he could see the morgue's drawers.

Marvin knew it was a brilliant idea now, the one he had lighting up inside his head like a thousand-watt light bulb. "We just need to make some movie magic."

VI
Catching a Killer

45
Saturday, 5:05 a.m.

MARVIN HAD IT ALL FIGURED OUT. Only his plan required the birds. He remembered what Bea had said: if you get Poe to move, the rest follow.

So he just talked to her, Poe, right outside the morgue, while Noah and Tori stood a few dozen feet away. Marvin wasn't sure if it would work, but he knew he needed the ravens. Now he felt vaguely like a fool for talking to a bird. Noah and Tori didn't seem to think it was foolish when he mentioned his idea, which made Marvin feel better.

He had new friends. Real friends. Spending the night on a haunted island with a murderer would do that.

Marvin said goodbye to Poe and rejoined his friends.

"Now what?" Noah asked. He hunched his shoulders inside his hoodie. Even under the shelter of the trees, it was freezing cold.

Marvin knew what he had to do next. "Now we set up at the cemetery. And then we have to get them all to show."

The plan was simple and complicated all at once. Simple, because the goal was straightforward, too: draw out the killer by scaring the heck out of them. Complicated in that everyone—all the suspects—had to show up in the same place.

At the same time. And the whole thing had to be scary.

But Marvin felt like he was the perfect person for that job. First off, he knew a thing or two about filming—even more now that he had been watching the *Ghost Catchers* crew. Secondly, he'd been scared many times over on this island.

And he had help from his friends.

Marvin hesitated, but then pulled Noah's notebook from his backpack. He saw Noah tense up.

Marvin said, careful to not sound like he was calling Noah out, "I know what this is."

Tori looked confused. Noah closed his eyes and looked like he was hoping Raven Island would swallow him whole.

Marvin said, "This is your book of fears, right, Noah?"

Noah nodded.

"I accidentally flipped back a few pages when I started taking notes yesterday," Marvin said. It seemed like a lifetime ago, but it was only last night. "I saw what you wrote, all these words . . ." He handed the book back to Noah. "I'm sorry you're afraid of so many things, dude. But I get it—a little bit, anyway."

Noah looked hopeful, like he was grateful someone finally understood him.

"I'm afraid all the time," Marvin said. "Not as much as you, but more than I let on. I'm afraid of the dark sometimes, of this island—heck, I'm even afraid of that creepy Mr. Thorne."

They all laughed at that, which cut right through the tension.

Noah clutched the notebook. "It helps to write it down. I have some catching up to do after this night."

"I'm afraid of a lot of things, too," Tori said. In a small voice, she went on, "I'm afraid my brother will be gone for years. I'm afraid he'll just be forgotten in that prison."

No one had words for that kind of fear.

Tori smacked her hands together, just like she always did at the beginning of a soccer game or when she was getting ready to defend penalty kicks. "Enough with the fear. Let's catch a killer."

Marvin nodded with determination.

Noah pulled out his notebook and flipped to a fresh page. "Okay, so how are we going to pull this off?"

"Are we sure we want to do this outside?" Tori asked. She glanced around the cemetery. "I get that it's creepy here, but inside it's easier for us to control the environment. Right?"

"You're right," Marvin said. He knew this from filming his short movies, too. "But we need the ravens to pull this off."

"Are you sure they'll show?" Noah asked. "They're birds, you know."

Marvin said with more certainty than he felt, "The ravens will be here."

Tori didn't look convinced but nodded anyway. "Okay. I trust you know your stuff. Let's write down the plan."

Marvin nodded. "First, we need to get everyone here. Ms. Chavez, Mr. Thorne, Bea, and the *Ghost Catchers* crew. Maybe we tell them we saw a ghost?"

"Bob's ghost!" Noah said with a smile.

"Yes!" Marvin grinned.

"But why would they even want to come?" Tori asked.

Marvin thought about that for a second. "Bob's ghost would be able to tell us who killed him. That will make the killer want to join us at the cemetery. The murderer will be afraid that Bob's ghost is going to tell the truth and reveal who shot him."

Tori added, "And maybe the rest of them will want to come, just to find out who the killer is."

"So how are we going to scare the killer enough to confess?" Noah asked, frowning.

Marvin sat on the short wall that surrounded the cemetery. It was funny: he wasn't even a little scared right now. But just the day before, this cemetery scared him to death. He said, "We need to write down all the ways *we* were scared since we got to Raven Island. And we can use all your fears from the notebook, Noah. We just need to use those fears for our plan."

They passed the notebook around. By the time they had written down all their fears and the scary moments they'd experienced on Raven Island, they had pages of notes to use. And Marvin had a list of things they had to gather to make it all work.

Marvin exhaled. He wasn't going to lie: he felt the pressure. This would be the greatest movie of all time. His directorial debut, if he shared this video. And not to mention the fact that they were drawing out a murderer. This was dangerous.

Marvin said, "Okay. We have to gather all these things." He tapped the notebook.

"I'll go to the mansion for what I can find," Tori said.

"We need costumes," Noah said. "I'll get those from the prison."

Marvin said, "I'll sneak the stuff we need to borrow from the *Ghost Catchers* crew."

Then they would set up. And it was showtime.

46
Saturday, 5:27 a.m.

TO GET TO THE PRISON, NOAH took one of the bicycles from the tunnel that went to the lighthouse. Now that he was alone, the tunnels felt a lot creepier than they were when he'd gone with Tori and Marvin. But Noah pushed the bike's pedals, knowing that Marvin was counting on his help.

It was nice to have a friend. Noah forgot how that felt. After the move, he'd left the few friends he had behind. He didn't realize how much he had missed having someone who had your back, and whose back you had in return.

And for just a little while, he didn't feel like his mom's death was looming over him like a dark cloud. He felt a little guilty about that—for forgetting his mom—but then it would make her happy to know that Noah had friends. And it would make his dad stop worrying about Noah so much.

As tired as Noah was, those thoughts gave him a boost of energy. He parked his bicycle near the prison's door, listening for voices up in the prison, at ground level. Sure enough, the team was there talking as Noah cracked the door. He paused and listened.

"Okay, let's analyze that footage from cell fourteen," Tammy said. Her footsteps were heavy.

Sarah said, "Not much from what I saw, but you never know." She didn't sound convinced. Or very excited. But then, it was five thirty in the morning, a hard time to be upbeat about anything other than sleep, especially when you'd been up all night.

Hatch's deep, somewhat loud voice went, "We *had* to have caught something! I felt the ghosts all around me. And our viewers won't settle for less."

"The viewers got a murder, didn't they?" Sarah said. "They should be happy with that for a while."

"Whoa," Hatch said. "No one wanted that guy dead—it's bad for business."

"That's not entirely true, is it?" Sarah said, biting back. "Do you even remember his name?"

"Um, sure, of course I do!" Hatch said, but it was obvious that he didn't. "He was our location scout, his name was . . . Billy?"

"Ha!" Sarah called. "See? Proof you don't care about anyone but yourself."

"Children, children," Tammy said very loudly. "Let's focus on the work, shall we?"

There was silence, other than the faint sound of tapping on a computer keyboard. Tammy, Sarah, and Hatch were all suspects in Bob's murder. They had been here, at the prison, when Bob was shot.

One of them could be the murderer.

Noah took a deep breath, remembering why he was here. He decided he could sneak upstairs and come up with some excuse to be at the guards' station. No one cared about a random kid anyway—that was his experience. Plus, they were too busy arguing up there.

Still, he was extra careful, making sure his sneakers made as little sound as possible. Noah climbed the stairs and held his breath as he walked the prison hall. The cells were empty, but there was an energy inside the prison. An electrical charge, brought on by the ghost hunters perhaps. Noah wanted to hurry up and leave already. But the costumes were in the guards' station at the center of the prison, right where the ghost-hunting team had set up their computer.

"Hi, kid," Hatch said as he passed Noah.

"Where are you going?" Tammy called after Hatch.

"Catching a smoke." Hatch's voice echoed off the empty prison walls. "You ladies are messing with my calm."

"Ha!" Sarah said.

But Tammy put a hand on Sarah's arm. "Leave him be," Tammy said.

"Hi, Noah," Sarah said, changing her focus but still looking angry. "What are you doing here?"

Noah hesitated. "Getting a costume. Mr. Thorne asked me to."

Tammy smiled. "That old grump. I don't know what is up with the guy, but it seems like he forgot how to smile. Like, *completely*."

Just a few hours ago, Noah would've agreed with her. But now that he knew the truth about the prison break, Mr. Thorne's sadness over the unlocked door, thinking he was part of the prison break somehow . . . Now Noah didn't think it was so odd that Mr. Thorne was grumpy.

But not being able to share this, he just shrugged.

Tammy and Sarah turned back to their screen. Noah went inside the guards' station and grabbed the costume. He remembered that's where he'd seen the gun, the one Bob was shot with. And he shivered. It was all surreal.

Then Noah walked back, trying not to make a sound.

"Say hi to Hatch on your way out!" Tammy called over her shoulder.

Noah had no intention of going that way. But he said, "Yeah, sure!"

Quietly, carefully, he went out through the side door, the one that led to the basement, and to the tunnel that led back to the cemetery. He peeked over his shoulder to make sure no one saw him.

Then he bumped right into Sarah. She'd snuck up on him.

"Hi, Noah," she said, looking straight into his eyes. Hers were a deep brown, the kind that cut right through you.

"Hi," Noah said, his voice a little shaky. He hoped she couldn't hear it. "How's ghost hunting?"

"Good," she said, taking a step back. "Great, in fact. We have a few hundred thousand new subscribers."

Noah couldn't tell if she sounded happy or sad about it. So he just nodded. Then he felt a little bold, after being so inspired by surviving a night on Raven Island. He asked, "Who do you think shot Bob?"

Sarah looked down at her shoes and exhaled. "He was here

to expose Raven Island's hidden locations and to try to find out what happened during the prison break, but . . . I don't know."

"Do you think that's why he was killed?" Noah asked.

Sarah said, "You should probably get out of here, kid. There's a murderer on the loose." She looked at Noah with those piercing eyes again, and Noah felt the hair on the back of his neck stand up.

What if Sarah was the killer? What if she had some reason to want Bob dead, some secret of her own? She had gotten him on the crew. She knew who he was. Maybe she'd brought him out here to kill him.

"I need to get back to work," Sarah said, walking past Noah. "Be safe out there."

Noah nodded, even though Sarah was already walking away from him.

He hurried down to the basement. He had to get away from here, and he had to take the tunnel. There was no time to walk through the woods, not if they were going to execute Marvin's plan before daybreak hit Raven Island.

Noah put Sarah at the top of his suspect list. She had to be the killer, even if he wasn't quite sure why.

He rushed down the hallway, through the secret door, and down the tunnel on his bicycle.

Noah could feel the air rush past his ears, and he felt an extra presence on the back of his bike.

"I'm proud of you," his mom said.

Noah froze as he reached the end of the tunnel. He was

afraid to turn around, afraid his mom would be gone.

"I miss you, Mom," he said, his throat tight.

"I know. But I'm always here," his mom said, her voice sounding like she was in an echo chamber. "Go find your friends."

Noah turned around to look at the back of the bike. To see his mom.

But she was gone.

47
Saturday, 5:30 a.m.

TORI WASN'T TOO CRAZY ABOUT GOING back to the mansion again. But there were things they needed from there, if Marvin's plan was going to work. She was excited about that part—the plan. But dread filled her shoes as she pushed the bike's pedals and until she reached the mansion's door.

Tori took a minute to brace herself, parking the bicycle. Why was she still so afraid of the warden's office? It wasn't like her brother was being held at *this* prison. If that were the case, she'd surely break him out.

There was that anger again. Tori knew that it did her no good—she had to *do* something to change things, not sit around and ball her fists until her nails made her palms bleed. She needed to put her anger to work—turn it into action. Useful action. Like helping Marvin with his plan to expose the killer.

Tori opened the door to the mansion and listened for any sounds of people. Tori was hoping that Mr. Thorne wasn't hovering nearby.

However, the other side of the door, inside the mansion, was dark and quiet. Dead quiet.

Tori went inside the basement and listened again—but once more, there was no sound. It was safe to go upstairs and get what she needed.

Tori exhaled in relief as she climbed the stairs. Now she just had to gather all the stuff Marvin asked for—it was a very specific list. And some of it was going to be hard to find . . .

First, she found the office. There was the warden's coat, hanging in the closet. Tori rolled it up and tucked it inside her backpack. The coat was dusty, and Tori had to stifle a sneeze.

Next, she moved on to the hard part: the baton in the frame. It looked barbaric, worn at the batting end. Tori felt sick to her stomach imagining all the inmates who had been beaten by this club. Who could do such a thing?

The back of the frame had some clips at the sides, which Tori undid. The wood backing came off, and Tori pulled the baton from the display.

Maybe they could burn it once this was all done. Tori smiled at that thought.

The next request from Marvin's list would have her going upstairs, to the bedroom. This also made Tori feel queasy, because Mr. Thorne had locked them inside that room. But she reminded herself that she was on a mission—no fear was allowed.

She opened the warden's office door. It was still very quiet out in the hallway.

Tori sneaked out, careful to close the door behind her, to leave things how she found them. Well, minus the warden's coat and his baton. Tori smiled to herself as she carefully, slowly climbed the stairs.

Take that, Raven Island Prison.

But really, she wished she could stick it to the prison her

brother was locked up in. Once she left Raven Island, Tori decided, she was going to do something. Visit her brother. Help with his legal defense—anything so he wasn't fighting alone.

Tori felt like a weight was lifted now that she knew what to do about missing Danny. She was going to help him.

But first: Marvin's plan.

Tori moved to the dresser and found the old nightgown inside. She took it, as well as the hair ribbons inside the wooden box.

She put both inside her backpack and turned around. Only to stare right at Ms. Chavez's face.

"What are you doing?' Ms. Chavez said.

Tori froze. But then she remembered to smile. "I came back for my phone. See?" She pulled it from her backpack. "I'd left it here, you know, earlier."

Ms. Chavez gave her a nod, which Tori took as permission to close her backpack.

"I should go find my friends," Tori muttered, smiling again. Ms. Chavez scared her, though Tori couldn't figure out why. Maybe it was because she could be the killer. Ms. Chavez had plenty of motivation: she had the secret of the tunnels to hide. And quite possibly, Ms. Chavez thought she was protecting her father's reputation.

"Have you seen him?" Ms. Chavez asked, her voice soft.

"Who?" Tori had no idea what Ms. Chavez was talking about, and she really wanted to get back to the cemetery.

"My father," Ms. Chavez said in a near whisper. "I was hoping . . . It is said that children are more likely to see a spirit, you see. And I was hoping that one of you three would see my father. Maybe you would be able to speak with his spirit and find out what happened."

"Not since we saw him at the docks." Tori was about to tell her that they figured out what happened, that Warden Chavez helped the prisoners escape through the tunnel to the mainland.

But then she realized what Ms. Chavez said. "You were only happy to keep us here, weren't you?" Tori asked, but she knew the answer.

Ms. Chavez had the tiniest smile on her lips. Like she was feeling pretty clever. But then she shook her head. "It was just a lucky break. Marvin made it so you stayed on Raven Island. I was trying to get to the ferry, but Mr. Thorne stopped me. My plan was to get a few of you kids—any of you, really—to stay the night."

"That's evil. It's kidnapping!" Tori said, feeling the journal cut into her waist. *Forget giving the journal back to her or telling her the truth,* Tori thought.

This woman was manipulative, evil!

"I just wanted to see my father," Ms. Chavez said again, softer this time.

Tori had to get out of there. Ms. Chavez was the killer, she had to be. Protecting Raven Island, her father—that was her motivation.

"I'm leaving," Tori said, pushing past Ms. Chavez.

Tori rushed down the stairs, almost tripping over Mr. Hitchcock near the office, rushing to get down to the basement. She didn't feel better until she got on the bike and hurried away from the mansion. She was so angry, and going so fast, she almost ran into Noah.

"Hey," he said, pulling up next to her. "Are you okay?"

"Fine," Tori said. She made herself exhale. "Let's go find Marvin. I want to catch this killer."

It was Ms. Chavez—Tori was sure of it.

And they would prove it soon enough.

48
Saturday, 5:45 a.m.

MARVIN HAD WALKED THE CEMETERY SEVERAL times now, planning his movie. It was going to be great—if everyone showed up, of course. He hoped that Tori and Noah would find what they needed.

Marvin sat down on the cemetery wall and realized that it was probably a little risky for any of them to be out there alone. In the tunnels. And then Marvin also realized something else:

He was all alone, in the dark. In a cemetery. On a haunted island.

Marvin took a deep breath to calm his nerves about the whole situation. But he was more nervous about his movie than about any hauntings on Raven Island at this point. The weather was doing that thing where it was super calm—the calm before the storm. Marvin felt the same about his movie.

The moon was even making an appearance through the clouds every now and then. It was a full moon.

But Marvin wasn't going to let his fear get to him. So what if there were a few hundred (or a few thousand?) dead people buried by his feet, right? That didn't mean that any ghosts were going to show up.

He thought of his grandma and all her Korean ghost stories.

And of his sisters, scaring him. He would have to tell them all about Raven Island and its gwishin—they'd get a kick out of it, Marvin thought.

Marvin whispered, "Ghosts, if you're going to show up, I beg you: wait about half an hour."

That was how long he figured it would take them to set up and get everyone to show up.

He'd snatched a power cord—he figured the *Ghost Catchers* crew left it behind in the lighthouse. The lights were rigged, and so were the speakers.

All of a sudden, Marvin thought about his old friend Kevin and how they used to plan fun stuff and pull pranks on others all the time. Marvin smiled. He missed those days and hoped Kevin had made friends at his new school. Marvin was glad to have his own new friends now. Not bad, even if he did have to spend a night on a haunted island, murder mystery included.

He hopped off the wall. And he was pretty sure he saw a shadow, past the mausoleum.

"Hold tight, ghosts," he said toward the back of the cemetery. "I'm going to need you to show up soon enough. All of you. Bring a friend—hey, bring all your friends! I'll bring my own for you to haunt."

"Yo, Marv—are you scaring the ghosts?" Tori called from the lighthouse. She laughed and joined Marvin near the cemetery.

"I figured I'd invite everyone," Marvin joked. "Did you get what we need?"

Tori nodded and dropped her backpack on the ground. "Though I'm not sure what the plan is with it all, exactly."

"I do, no worries." Marvin unpacked Tori's bag just as Noah joined them, too.

"I got everything," Noah said. "Now what?"

Marvin smiled, "Now we set the stage. This is going to be the scariest movie Raven Island has ever seen."

They strung up the vines as a booby trap. Noah wore the prison guard's uniform, and Tori wore the nightgown to pretend to be a patient from the sanatorium. They were posing as ghosts, hoping to scare the killer into confessing. The stage was set, but Marvin felt nervous.

What if it didn't work?

Tori, Noah, and Marvin had been sure to invite everyone: Hatch, Sarah, and Tammy. Ms. Chavez and Mr. Thorne—even resident bird lady Bea was asked to join them at the cemetery.

We saw something. Something strange. Maybe it was Bob's ghost, trying to tell us who killed him . . .

That was what the three kids told everyone. And that was all anyone needed to hear.

Hatch and his crew wanted to catch a ghost.

Ms. Chavez and Mr. Thorne wanted to hear from a specific ghost: Warden Chavez.

And bird expert Bea? Well, she just wanted to see what the hubbub was all about. She was a curious one, after all, like the birds. And who knew? Maybe she wanted Bob dead . . .

One of the six adults on the island was a killer. And Marvin, Noah, and Tori were determined to draw this person out.

Marvin even decided on a title for his movie.

The Killer Trap.

49
Saturday, 6:20 a.m.

"IT WAS A DARK AND STORMY night," Marvin said, starting his narration. He wanted his introduction to be like the one he'd seen Jordan Peele do on *The Twilight Zone*. Serious. Dramatic. Ghostly.

The rain was drizzling, and the wind whipped around Marvin, as if he had planned it this way. It was cold, but his excitement for the movie kept Marvin warm.

Would they be able to pull this off?

Noah held the camera far enough away for the lens to catch Marvin in the warden's jacket, but close enough so no one else would ruin the shot. They would be able to stream live, as long as Sarah, Tammy, and Hatch didn't catch on. But Noah, Tori, and Marvin figured the *Ghost Catchers* crew had to be walking in the woods right now. The three kids had the advantage of the tunnels and the bicycles: they could beat all the suspects to the cemetery. Even Ms. Chavez and Mr. Thorne could only go so fast in their golf cart through the forest.

Marvin continued for the audience online, "Somewhere on Raven Island, there is a killer. A killer who thought they were keeping their crime a secret. But the island has a mind of its own. It will not release any of its visitors without the truth, the whole truth, and nothing but the truth." Marvin raised the warden's leather-bound journal. "Welcome to Raven Island."

Noah panned out. And turned off the camera with a huge grin on his face.

Tori smiled, too. "That was good, Marvin."

Marvin felt adrenaline rush through his veins. Let's face it: it was the only thing keeping him awake. "You think anyone is tuning in?" he asked as he handed Tori the journal.

"No way to tell without checking the computer back at the prison," Tori said. "But knowing how everyone was tuning in after the murder . . . I would say we have an audience."

Noah froze. "I think I hear voices. We have to get set up." He handed Marvin the camera. All around them, the rain was whipping, as if nature wanted them to take their places for the performance. The sun would be up soon—the late-night darkness made everything look extra ghostly.

"Welcome to the Twilight Zone," Marvin said, mostly to himself. It felt like he was in a *Twilight Zone* episode, here on Raven Island. Now it was time to make his own show . . .

Both Noah and Tori took their places. Marvin set the camera on the tripod and waited until he saw the white golf cart speeding its way on the forest path.

"They're here!" Marvin whispered. He turned on the camera.

Showtime.

The graveyard was quiet again, which no longer creeped Marvin out at all. He was comfortable hanging with the ghosts of Raven Island. What made him nervous was this killer.

Who killed Bob? They would find out before daybreak . . .

The pine needles on the path crunched under the weight of the golf cart's tires. Ms. Chavez muttered as she got off the golf cart, "What's this about, then?"

Mr. Thorne just shrugged.

And Marvin was pretty sure he saw the ghost of John Bellini behind the cemetery, between the trees. He looked so real . . .

Then, as if they'd timed it, Hatch, Tammy, and Sarah came walking up, too. Tammy carried a camera, but under her arm. Hatch had his cell phone out.

"If there are any spirits with us tonight, please show yourself," Hatch said. "*Please*, come on." He sounded tired, and like he was begging. Marvin guessed by the tone of his voice that Raven Island hadn't been a good ghost-hunting expedition.

But that was about to change.

First, the lighthouse shone its bright light and turned the beam, like it was a floodlight from the prison.

"Whoa," Tammy said, and stepped back.

"Who did that?' Ms. Chavez called toward the lighthouse.

Just as quickly, the light turned off. Leaving everyone to rub their eyes, blinded by the brightness. Everyone but Marvin and Tori, who were prepared and kept their eyes on the ground.

It was Noah who was inside the lighthouse, making the light work via the unstable electric current it got.

Marvin could see the pine trees swaying in the wind. And Bea was there, up on a branch in a pine tree. Watching.

"Bob, are you here?" Sarah asked. She had the voice recorder out in front of her. Her eyes were hopeful. The *Ghost Catchers* crew all walked in line.

Suddenly, there was a quick *swoosh* sound—and the vines that Marvin, Noah, and Tori had strung up as a booby trap had all three ghost hunters stumbling and falling. Right onto the gravestones.

"*Aaarghhh!*" Sarah called.

Hatch hollered, "I'm on a dead person! Get it off me!"

Tammy got to her feet first and helped Sarah, then a grumpy Hatch, to their feet. "What was that?" Tammy asked. She looked down only to find air and graveyard soil. Noah had been quick, pulling the vines away from his spot near the giant oak tree.

"It's the ghosts of Raven Island," Marvin said. "They won't rest until the killer reveals themself . . ." Marvin hoped he sounded ghostly.

From the looks on everyone's faces, he was successful. The ghost hunters looked pale, tired, and, most importantly, scared.

But not the ghost of John Bellini. He kept coming closer and closer still. And Marvin was beginning to wonder . . .

What if he wasn't a ghost at all? What if this was John Bellini, alive and in the flesh?

Only Marvin didn't have time to think about this too much. His plan was in action and moving along.

Down the dark graveyard, next to the mausoleum, there was a white apparition. A woman in a nightgown—who was actually Tori, of course, wearing the nightgown she took from the mansion's bedroom.

"Are you getting this, Tammy?" Hatch whispered.

But Tammy had dropped her camera near the cemetery entrance. And she was backing out between the gravestones. "I'm outta here," she muttered. "I'm no killer, and I don't like this place."

Ms. Chavez stepped closer, curious rather than scared. But she hesitated in the middle of the graveyard. "Are you here, Dad?" she whispered very softly.

That's when Noah appeared, wearing a prison costume. "The dead want answers," he whispered in a ghostly voice. Any other time, Marvin was sure they'd be revealed as fakes. But in the darkness of the graveyard, the clouds covering the moon, and with all the Raven Island lore . . .

It looked scary. But was it scary enough to reveal the killer?

Then there were some unexpected guests. The faceless prisoners they'd seen the day before—all six appeared, holding their shovels. Glancing at the crowd, then inching closer. And closer.

Marvin had to stifle a scream.

Ms. Chavez stepped back, scared by the faceless prisoners, the dalgyal gwishin. And perhaps by Noah's ghostly appearance, too. She stumbled over Mr. Hitchcock, the cat, who scurried into the forest.

Mr. Thorne tried to take Ms. Chavez's elbow, but caught air. "I will tell you the truth, Ms. Chavez, I promise," he said in a near whisper.

There was a whistle that was getting louder and louder. Joseph Fink, the Birdman of Raven Island, stood near the mausoleum, with a ghost bird perched on his right hand.

Then there was the sound of a bouncing ball, banging against the back of the mausoleum. A rhythmic bounce, over and over.

Bang. Bang. It sounded like a prisoner bouncing a tennis ball off the wall.

Of course, it was Tori with her stress ball. But the adults stood straight, frozen in fear.

Hatch was hanging back, having Sarah take the lead as usual.

Sarah called, "Bob? Are you here?"

The sound of the bouncing ball stopped. Then Tori set off her phone, making ghostly howling noises.

"Tell us who killed you, Bob," Sarah said, looking for her friend's ghost with tears running down her face. "Please."

The faceless prisoners stood frozen, like they weren't sure what to do. And that old prisoner's ghost, John Bellini, was walking past them, through them, like he didn't care.

That's when Marvin heard voices. It sounded like when he was up in his room and his parents were having a party downstairs. Like a whole bunch of voices speaking at once, but you couldn't hear what they were saying.

This wasn't part of their plan. Where were these voices coming from?

Slowly, there was another voice. One that got louder and louder. "Confess!" it said.

And louder still: *"Confess!"* Over and over, the voice called for the killer to admit their crime.

"Confess! CONFESS!" It came from all around the forest now. All thirteen ravens, calling out.

John Bellini smiled. "Very well." Then he pulled out a gun.

Mr. Thorne said, "You're alive."

He nodded. "That's me. And you're supposed to be dead, Mr. Thorne."

50
Saturday, 6:29 a.m.

JUST LIKE THAT, THE VOICES STOPPED. The cemetery was quiet.

Mr. Thorne looked at his hands and body, which suddenly seemed just a little . . . fuzzy.

"Wait," Marvin said. "You're a ghost, Mr. Thorne?"

Mr. Thorne looked shocked. "I suppose I am . . ."

Tori said, "It all makes sense now: the way he would sneak up on people and didn't eat at dinner, and . . . well, you look pale as a ghost, Mr. Thorne."

John Bellini, still wielding a gun, nodded. "I shot him with his own gun, outside the tunnel to the mainland."

"There's a tunnel to the mainland?" Hatch asked. "That would've been way easier with the equipment . . ."

"Wait—aren't you a ghost?" Noah asked John Bellini.

But he just smiled. "I just let you think I was. And quite effectively so."

"You killed Bob!" Sarah exclaimed.

John Bellini said, "I came here last week, with the delivery crew. That's when I heard about you ghost hunters coming here, and I knew I had to plan ahead. I couldn't have anyone poking around—like you kids did." He waved the gun at Marvin, Tori, and Noah. "Or you might find out the truth about our escape and about me killing Mr. Thorne here. That would have me facing a fresh murder charge, with a new bounty on my head. And today, with technology, it's a lot harder to hide from authorities. So I came back. With firepower."

Tori said, still wearing the nightgown, "We saw you, on the docks."

John Bellini nodded. "I caught the ghost of the warden. Tried to tell him to stay away from everyone and keep the island's secret, or I'd kill his precious little girl."

Ms. Chavez looked livid. "I'm not so little anymore."

John Bellini said, "You're still the most important thing to him."

"Why kill Bob?" Sarah asked.

Bellini answered, "He found the doors to the tunnels and started to make the connection. But I guess the truth is out now."

"What about the other escaped prisoners?" Noah asked. "Did you kill them, too?"

Bellini shook his head. "No need. We all got out on the other side and went our separate ways. The brothers Smith ended up somewhere down south. We never got along—they were annoying do-gooders, always looking for ways to make up for their crimes." Bellini rolled his eyes. "So I went my own way. But I kept tabs on them.

"I've been living quietly up north—and I only committed a few crimes, when it was necessary. I wish you had just left the island in peace, Ms. Chavez."

Ms. Chavez looked livid, but also had her eyes on the gun.

There was a silence, then Bellini said, "Now I'm gonna have to figure out what to do with you all. Not enough bullets in this gun." He flashed an evil grin, and Marvin saw his brown teeth.

But then Marvin also saw Mr. Thorne. He was mad as anything and had drifted to the back.

Then Mr. Thorne charged. With all his might. And he ran John Bellini down.

Ms. Chavez rushed to grab the gun and put her boot on one of Bellini's arms. Hatch got his legs, and Tori, the other arm.

John Bellini wasn't going anywhere.

Noah took a set of cuffs from his warden getup. "This is coming in handy."

Marvin smiled. And he turned off the camera.

51
Saturday, 6:50 a.m.

HATCH AND SARAH TOOK JOHN BELLINI back to the prison, so he could be taken into custody once the ferry came. Tammy stayed behind to gather all the equipment that Marvin, Tori, and Noah had borrowed. But none of the *Ghost Catchers* crew seemed too mad about that—they got the episode of a lifetime, after all.

And as if Marvin planned it that way, between the trees, there was another apparition. It was faint, and faraway, but Marvin was sure it was a dead man's ghost.

Bob's ghost. He looked at Marvin, Tori, and Noah, and gave them the smallest nod. As if to say: *Thank you.* The unfinished business of his murder was done. He could rest in peace now.

"Everyone—look!" Marvin said, calling over his shoulder. But when he turned back around, Bob's ghost was gone. "Never mind," Marvin muttered. He hoped he got it on film.

"That was something else, you guys," Tammy said, elbowing Marvin. "We'll have to talk later—I wanna know how you pulled that off!"

Tori, Noah, and Marvin agreed.

Marvin exhaled. They did it.

Over the horizon behind them, the sun was coming up,

brightening the cemetery. It was a new day on Raven Island. The storm had passed, and it looked like it might actually be sunny. Marvin was about to mention it when he saw Mr. Hitchcock walking toward the lighthouse.

And he was pretty sure he saw the ghost of another man in a warden's uniform. The warden's ghost bent down to pet the cat, then looked over toward Marvin.

Marvin turned toward Ms. Chavez to tell her, hoping the ghost of Warden Chavez wasn't gone by the time he did. But Marvin didn't need to worry. The warden's daughter saw her father, if only for a second, and waved to him just before he disappeared, as the sun came up.

"Was that . . . ?" Noah whispered next to Marvin.

"It was," Tori said softly, as if she were afraid to break the spell.

Ms. Chavez wiped her cheeks. "I was right. It was you children who brought him here."

Marvin wasn't so sure—after all, Mr. Thorne was a ghost and had been seen by everyone. But Marvin nodded all the same. Ms. Chavez got what she wanted, and so did he, Tori, and Noah.

Mr. Thorne hung around, looking awkward.

"You're still here, Mr. Thorne," Noah said. "I thought once a ghost was at peace, they would disappear."

Tammy said, "I've seen this kind of thing at other haunted places we've investigated. Mr. Thorne is tied to the island. He needs to stay."

Mr. Thorne nodded. "It's my duty to care for Raven Island."

Marvin turned and looked toward the trees. "The voices . . ."

"That was all the ravens," Bea said. Again, she'd sneaked up on him, out of nowhere. "They can mimic human voices."

Marvin added, "I asked Poe to say 'Confess!' It seemed scary and ghostly." He smiled. "And of course, she brought her twelve friends."

Ms. Chavez asked, "Now it's your turn, Mr. Thorne: What secret are you hiding from me?"

52
Saturday, 7:52 a.m.

TORI WAS ANXIOUS AS THEY STOOD inside the morgue entry, surrounded by all the pictures. They were waiting for Mr. Thorne, who was helping Hatch and Sarah lock John Bellini in one of the prison cells.

Marvin and Noah sat on the morgue's floor, going over the video footage with Tammy.

But Tori couldn't sit still, even though she was bone-tired from being up all night. She couldn't help thinking of her brother again, and of all the prisoners who had lived on Raven Island, who'd suffered, forgotten on this rock. It wasn't right.

She stood in front of the framed photograph of Warden Chavez, surrounded by all the prisoners.

"He hated it here," Ms. Chavez said as she joined Tori. "Even as a young girl, I knew that." She pointed to three of the prisoners who were standing at the back, almost imperceptible. "That's the brothers Smith and John Bellini."

All this time, they'd thought they saw John Bellini's ghost in the forest and by the dock. He turned out to be alive and well. It was just a replay of the old events, Hatch had explained. And Mr. Thorne turned out to be a ghost!

Raven Island sure was a strange place.

Tori asked, "Where do you think the other two prisoners went?"

Ms. Chavez said with a smile, "Hopefully, somewhere good. The decades they spent on Raven Island were punishment enough for their crimes—and I think my father thought so, too. Given that no one heard from these escaped prisoners again, I'm not sure where they disappeared to."

Tori paused and perked up, as if she'd realized something important. "I read on the website of the prisoners' families that some of them received postcards from the Smith brothers. And the two of them showed up at a funeral in disguise. What if that really was them?"

Ms. Chavez shrugged. "Perhaps it doesn't matter. These men would be in their eighties or nineties now. If they're still alive."

"Let's hope so," Tori said. She took the journal from her waistband. "I'm sorry I kept this all night. I should have given it to you right away." She handed the leather-bound book to Ms. Chavez. "I found this in your office, at the warden's mansion. It's your father's journal."

Ms. Chavez's eyes fogged up. "Oh, thank you." She clutched the journal. "I miss him, you know."

Tori thought of her brother Danny, whom she hadn't seen in months. "I can only imagine."

The door to the morgue swung open and Mr. Thorne walked in, bringing with him a waft of cold air and the smell of cigarette smoke. "John Bellini is locked up but not too happy about it."

"Good," Ms. Chavez said as she put the journal inside her bag. "Now, show me this secret."

Mr. Thorne walked them all down to the basement. And to the second locked door.

"You told me it was a storage room, Mr. Thorne," Ms. Chavez said, perturbed. "You said the key was lost."

"I lied," Mr. Thorne said as he unlocked the door. "I thought I was protecting you. And your mother, and Warden Chavez's legacy."

Mr. Thorne showed her the tunnel. He told Ms. Chavez the whole story: how he'd found the door unlocked on the night of the prison break, and how shortly afterward the warden was found dead. How everyone thought the escaped prisoners had drowned and the warden tried to retrieve the boat.

Mr. Thorne said, "John Bellini shot me and dragged my body into the woods. I remember now, but I . . . I think I just decided to forget, so I didn't have to accept that I'm dead."

That certainly made sense. The whole story was awful, Tori thought.

Mr. Thorne went on, "I knew that if anyone discovered the truth about that day, you and your mother would be cast out. And you'd be left with no money," Mr. Thorne said to Ms. Chavez as they stood in the tunnel. "So I didn't tell anyone. And when they closed the prison, I just kept the keys I had to myself. For fifty years . . ." Mr. Thorne had silent tears running down his cheeks.

"You've been alone on a forgotten island, Mr. Thorne," Ms.

Chavez said. "And since we never met during my short time on the island as a child . . . I didn't realize you were a ghost."

"I had to protect the secret," Mr. Thorne said softly.

"So you mean that this whole time we could've walked back to the mainland?" Tammy asked, her loud voice echoing off the walls. "Do you know how seasick I got on that ferry?"

That made Mr. Thorne laugh, which was possibly a first in fifty years. Mr. Thorne said, "No. The tunnel collapsed not long after the prison closed down."

"That sounds like a new project, then," Ms. Chavez said. Then she turned to Mr. Thorne. "Thank you for protecting me and my mother. That secret must've been a heavy burden."

They hugged, which Tori would never have imagined either was capable of. Especially since Mr. Thorne was a ghost. But then, this night on Raven Island had left everyone changed.

Ms. Chavez and Mr. Thorne got caught up in conversation as they all went back upstairs and into the morgue's waiting room once again. By the time Ms. Chavez glanced at her watch, she startled and grabbed Tori's arm. "Oh my," she said. "We'd better rush."

Marvin looked at his phone and hurried toward the door. "Tori, Noah—come on! It'll be ten o'clock soon."

And Tori realized: if they didn't hurry, they were going to miss the ferry. Again. Which would be the craziest thing, since that's what she'd been waiting for all night.

Tori actually laughed. At last, they were going home.

EPILOGUE
Six months later . . .

"*AAAAANNNND* . . . CUT!" MARVIN CALLED. HE PUT his phone down with a smile. Tori breathed a sigh of relief. This prison costume was pretty uncomfortable, never mind the fake blood that was oozing from her mouth.

But nothing could ruin Tori's mood, not today. She'd stumble around the Raven Island morgue all day if she had to.

Thankfully, they were done. Tori wiped her mouth and walked over to Marvin. They had been filming all morning—with Ms. Chavez's permission, of course. Mr. Thorne and Ms. Bea had even played a part in the earlier scenes. Mr. Thorne, as a real-life ghost, just got a little fuzzy around the edges sometimes.

Marvin's sisters had helped with some of the scenes, too—they were really proud of Marvin. His grandma contributed by telling Korean ghost stories. Marvin realized they made for great movie material, and his grandma seemed to enjoy being part of the whole thing.

"How's it looking?" Tori asked.

Marvin smiled. "Awesome. With some editing, a few changes . . ."

Noah groaned. "Don't tell me we have to come back here again!" He put down the flashlight. "This is the third time already!"

Marvin grinned even wider. "Just kidding. We're done." He turned off his phone. "I'll have a lot of editing to do, but I think I can get it done in time, before the Indie MovieFest contest deadline."

"That's awesome, Marvin," Tori said. She used some wipes to clean her face. "Let us know when it's done."

Noah nodded. "And I'll help." Marvin and Noah were movie buddies now, often spending long afternoons at Marvin's house to edit movies or write scripts. It wasn't Tori's thing—she'd rather play soccer any day—but she'd often drop by after practice to help, or just hang out. Things had been good since they spent that cold night catching a killer (and a few ghosts).

They were true friends now. You couldn't survive a night on Raven Island together and not share a bond, Tori thought.

She'd also gotten closer to Ms. Chavez—strangely, since Tori couldn't stand the island owner that night after the field trip. But Tori found a kindred spirit in her quest to make a change. What happened to her brother was wrong, and Tori's blood boiled every time she thought about Danny, and to the other prisoners jailed for things they didn't do, or locked away and forgotten by the world even if they did commit a crime. Even a guy like John Bellini deserved to be treated with dignity.

Ms. Chavez thought so, too, and she vowed to pick up where her father had left off when it came to the desire to change things. She was an activist for prison reform, using her lawyer status to help the Innocence Project—an organization that helped people convicted of a crime they didn't commit—

and different organizations fight mass incarceration.

They were big goals, and Tori often felt overwhelmed by it all. How was she supposed to make a difference? But Ms. Chavez sometimes let her come along when she was making a speech or talking to legislators, and that made Tori feel like she could do something. By talking about her brother and how his being in prison had impacted her. By sharing her story.

Today wasn't about any of that, though.

"Come on, guys—the ferry will be here soon!" Tori called to Marvin and Noah. They disappeared into the morgue's basement, through the opening that no longer had a door. Ms. Chavez wanted everything out in the open, including the tunnels. *No more doors with locks*, she'd said.

Tori liked that, a lot.

"We're still early," Marvin said behind her.

"I just don't want to be late," Tori said. Especially not today.

She and Noah rode the bikes, racing to get to the prison side, laughing the whole way.

They parked their bikes and made their way up into the prison.

"Oh, good, you're here," Mr. Thorne said from his spot in the guards' station. Ever since he told the secret he'd been carrying for fifty years—that he had known the prisoners escaped through the secret tunnel to the mainland—to Ms. Chavez, he seemed to be lighter on his feet. Or maybe that was just because everyone knew he was a ghost now. But now that Mr. Thorne was no longer grumpy about everything, he actually turned out to be a pretty funny guy. Plus, he knew all of Raven Island's history, which helped Marvin make his movie.

"Hey, Mr. Thorne," Tori said. "We're actually on our way to see the ferry arrive."

"Of course," Mr. Thorne said. Then he tossed her a ball of fabric. "Here, since you kids were the original overnight tour group." He threw Noah and Marvin balls, too.

When they unrolled them, Tori saw that they were T-shirts.

I SURVIVED THE NIGHT . . . ON RAVEN ISLAND, it said on the front. There was a picture of the prison on it, with a raven near the bottom.

They all put the T-shirts on for Mr. Thorne, who looked . . . happy. Smiling. "Looks amazing," he said. "I can't wait to start the tours next month." Mr. Thorne was working on a nighttime ghost-hunting tour.

Poe was not happy about it. Tori could tell when they walked outside. The raven sat on the picnic bench, trotting from this claw to that one.

"It'll be okay, Poe," Tori whispered as they passed her. "Don't worry. You can always scare those tourists away, right?"

They rushed toward the ferry dock, though it was still far out, having just left the mainland.

But Tori wanted to watch it arrive. It got closer, and closer, until she could see him at the front of the ferry, right where she had sat with Marvin and Noah just six months ago.

Her brother Danny. Even from afar, Tori could see that he was smiling.

Tori waved. And she felt like everything would be okay now.

A NOTE FROM THE AUTHOR

I HOPE YOU ENJOYED READING *Daybreak on Raven Island*! As I started writing the book, I really set out to simply write a ghostly book with a good murder mystery—but as I was writing, it became clear that there was more to the story than a ghostly island. There was an old prison and a girl with a broken heart over her brother's incarceration.

I am by no means an expert on prison reform. Research is part of a writer's job, however, and the more I dug into the way prisons are run today, the more my heart broke right along with Tori's.

As I'm writing this, the United States has the largest percentage of imprisoned people in the world—in fact, we have five times more incarcerated people per capita (that means per citizen) than any other country in the world. Even if someone didn't commit a crime, just like Tori's brother Danny, unless they have money for bail, they're often stuck in a slow-moving system that is designed to keep people locked up. Especially Black people like Noah and his family, or Asian people like Marvin, which makes the system even more unjust.

There are a lot of statistics and facts I could go on about, but maybe the best thing is to sum it up: The prison system hurts a lot of people. And there are companies that make a profit off it, resulting in horrible situations just like Tori's brother not even being able to call home.

So what does that even mean for a kid like you? Simply put, one in twenty-eight kids has an incarcerated parent—that means there's likely someone in your class or in your grade who is affected by it. And like Tori, those kids may have a hard time talking about it. It's important that we don't forget about people in jail or prison, or about their families struggling with all the stresses that come with incarceration. *No one gets left behind*—it's a good motto for Tori's soccer team, but just as important in life.

Tori and Ms. Chavez are trying to make a change in the book, as are some great organizations in real life. Education is power, so if your heart broke a little with Tori, too, find out more about the current state of affairs and how you can help at the following resources (with your parent's or guardian's permission, of course):

- American Civil Liberties Union's page on prisoners' rights: aclu.org/issues/prisoners-rights
- The Innocence Project: innocenceproject.org
- Equal Justice Initiative: eji.org
- Children of Incarcerated Parents Partnership: coipp.org/resources
- Youth of Incarcerated Parents Resources: youth.gov/youth-topics/children-of-incarcerated-parents